"I abandoned my baby"

Suddenly a line magicked itself into the round window as if from nowhere. Then, moments later, I watched goggle-eyed as a line appeared in the square window as well. I swallowed hard in an attempt to force my heart from my throat back down into my chest, and leant heavily against the toilet door for support. This was unreal!

I was absolutely stunned. *This can't be happening to me!* I thought. *Surely I'll wake up in a minute and realize this whole day has been a horrible dream?* But I knew that wasn't going to happen, I knew deep down that I'd been ignoring something that had been staring me in the face weeks ago.

"I abandoned my baby"

Sue Dando

SCHOLASTIC

Scholastic Children's Books
Commonwealth House, 1–19 New Oxford Street,
London WC1A 1NU, UK
A division of Scholastic Ltd
London ~ New York ~ Toronto ~ Sydney ~ Auckland
Mexico City ~ New Delhi ~ Hong Kong

First published in the UK by Scholastic Ltd, 1999

Copyright © Sue Dando, 1999

ISBN 0 439 01009 8

Typeset by Falcon Oast Graphic Art
Printed by Cox and Wyman Ltd, Reading, Berks.

10 9 8 7 6 5 4 3 2 1

Prologue

For everyone else in the family, this is just like any other Saturday evening. Dad, my sister Shona and I are sitting at the kitchen table eating runny eggs and McCain's oven chips, and the only noise to be heard is the TV droning away in the background. No one speaks – we rarely do at meal times. We're not like one of those families you see on telly soaps, who seem to spend all their time sitting around a big table of food and getting into huge discussions about every aspect of their lives, exposing their thoughts and feelings in the most minute detail. "Pass the tomato sauce, please," just about sums up the extent of our tea-time conversations, feeding our faces being much more important in the Hamilton household.

Today, eating is way down on my list of priorities. I absent-mindedly push burnt chips around my plate and stare bleakly into the gooey splodge of egg that is spilling its yellow insides all over the plate. Life can't get much worse than this, I think grimly, blinking furiously as I try to force back the tears which are threatening to escape from my clouding eyes. I feel like a complete fraud, sitting here with my family, pretending nothing is wrong, when in fact nothing is right.

I stare blankly through the TV set, vaguely listening to the theme tune as the local news comes on. My mind begins registering what the headline story is and suddenly I am sitting bolt upright and taking notice.

A newborn baby girl has been found abandoned on the doorstep of a doctor's surgery in Middleton Road, reports the newscaster's voice.

I gasp out loud and feel the colour drain from me as I watch the screen. My body feels icy cold. The woman reporter goes on to say how the baby was discovered by an employee who'd arrived to open the surgery, and has been taken to the local hospital where she is being cared for by staff. Doctors say she is less than a day old.

My heart breaks as I look at the film of the tiny baby lying in a nurse's arms. She is pink and wrinkle-free, with a mop of black hair and amazing cobalt blue eyes that look quietly out from the TV screen, blissfully unaware of the predicament she is in. The report concludes with an appeal from the police for the mother to come forward, then cuts back to the studio and the next story.

I am no longer listening. Months of pent up emotion and abject despair spill out of me as I burst into tears and run from the room. You see, the baby on the TV screen is mine.

Chapter 1

"Please tell me, Tim, *please*! You know how much I hate surprises. Can't you just give me a little clue? Go on, you know you want to."

Edging a little closer to him on the sofa we were sharing in his mum's living-room, I grabbed hold of Tim's sleeve and gave it an insistent tug. I had on my most pleading face, eyes imploring him like a lost puppy. And all because I was desperate for him to tell me what he'd bought me for Christmas.

I knew I was being pathetic, but I really did hate surprises and it was also very unusual for him not to have spilt the beans by now. Tim couldn't keep a secret to save his life. In the two years we'd been going out together, there wasn't one Christmas or birthday where I didn't know at least three weeks in advance what he'd bought for me. He couldn't help himself. We'd got into a routine whereby as soon as he'd bought the said gift, he would insist that I try and guess what it was. And when I invariably couldn't, like a big kid he would just *have* to tell me. Sometimes he was so thrilled by what he'd purchased he couldn't even wait until the big day to hand it over, suggesting I open it *right now* because "it won't matter if it's a bit early".

But this year was different. There was just one week to go before Christmas and so far Tim had said nothing. It had got to the stage where I'd been forced to drop some not very subtle hints, like, "I was thinking of buying the new Prodigy CD. Unless, that is, you've already got it me for Christmas." To which he asked if he could borrow it. Hmm.

After much deliberation, I finally came to the heart-stopping conclusion that maybe – just maybe – he wasn't saying anything because this year he was getting me the ultimate present: an engagement ring.

I truly thought I would die of happiness if Tim asked me to marry him. We were perfect for each other, I knew that almost from the beginning. We just clicked. Everything felt right between us, it always had done. I firmly believed that we were meant to be together for ever. Admittedly, we both felt we were too young to get married now – he's eighteen, I'm seventeen – but we figured that once we both had our careers up and running we would make that all-important commitment to each other and eventually – maybe in another ten years or so – start a family.

That was the plan. And it wasn't only *my* fantasy. Many times in the past Tim and I had often had lengthy conversations about where we'd live, the cars we'd drive, the fabulous careers we'd have. And we always assumed we'd do everything together, as a couple.

So the prospect of him presenting me with an engagement ring and a proposal (on bended knee and with a rose in his mouth like they do in romantic comedies, perhaps?) on Christmas morning filled me with a kind of tingling anticipation which had been building up ever since the notion hit me while I was lying in the bath one evening. And which was now – understandably, I think – becoming completely unbearable.

I pulled playfully at Tim's sleeve once more and studied his face, looking for clues. I needn't have bothered since he was staring intently at the television screen, engrossed in some tedious football match or other.

I felt the muscles on my face soften and relax, and the corners of my mouth turn up into an involuntary smile of contentment and pleasure as I watched him. I never got tired of looking at him and wondered if there would be a time when I didn't fancy him. I doubted it. He wasn't what you would call conventionally handsome, but he had the kind of looks that were cute in a boyish sort of way. He was cute aged six (I've seen the photos that prove it) and I imagined he would be equally cute aged sixty. He had that sort of face.

He had big blue eyes and the longest blond eyelashes that most girls would die for. He had slightly crooked front teeth and a cheeky, cheesy grin that made him look like a bit of a tearaway, although in fact he wasn't, instead being hard-working and bright and determined to get on. His hair was sandy-coloured and straight, cut in a trendy short style. He was tall and skinny, but not in a geeky way, and had a pert bum that he sometimes jokingly referred to as his best asset. He was totally adorable.

My mind wandered again as I recalled the first time I had set eyes on him. It was in the dinner hall at school. My best friend at the time, Zoë, and I were tucking into doughy school-baked pizzas and gossiping about and/or eyeing up any lads who happened to be in the vicinity (like you do when it's lunchtime and you're bored and have nothing better to do other than your dull English homework which is due in next lesson).

We'd long since decided that the best thing about going to a school with over 2500 students was the fact that there was always previously unspotted talent to be on the look-out for.

This proved to be the case when I noticed a seriously fit guy sauntering through the hall with another lad. They were obviously having a laugh together because the Seriously Fit Guy's face suddenly cracked into the broadest grin, then he laughed out loud. As he cackled away he looked around the hall and must have caught sight of me gawping at him. He cracked an even broader grin, winked at me, then looked away and said something to his mate who, leering, scanned the room in my direction, then muttered something back. Laughing, they disappeared out of sight around a corner and I was left with a big slab of pizza raised halfway to my mouth and a starry look in my eyes.

From then on I made sure I went out of my way to look for Tim — that was the divine name of the Seriously Fit Guy — around school, and it didn't take long to work out his routine, and to make sure mine began to mirror it. Putting myself about like this (so to speak) obviously worked, because within a couple of weeks of first setting eyes on him, we were hanging out together as friends, though, as I found out later, we both had ulterior motives. We hit it off straight away, which was weird in a way – I felt so at ease with him, it was like I'd known him all my life. No one was surprised when we started going out together.

Ours had become an all-consuming relationship as our lives entwined and we began spending more time together, slowly becoming a couple with one life rather than two. I saw less of Zoë and my other girlfriends; instead, Tim and I did everything together, went everywhere as boyfriend and girlfriend.

As far as I was concerned, nothing much had changed since then. Our relationship seemed to get stronger as the weeks, months and years passed. Sure we'd had our ups and downs, but who hasn't? If anything, I felt the downs made us stronger as a couple.

Take now, for example. Tim had been pretty grumpy with life in recent times, and if I didn't know him better than I knew myself, I would be worried. I'd think something was up. But Tim was in his final year at school. He was revising hard for three A levels because he was desperate to get into a good university to study law. He was terrified that he was going to fail his exams; he was under pressure and I sometimes felt like he was taking his pent-up frustrations and tensions out on me.

We'd had a couple of humdinging rows in the last couple of months, more often than not sparked off by something really trivial, like me being fifteen minutes late for a night out at the cinema so that we missed the first five minutes of a film. Or Tim agreeing to go to a gig with me then crying off at the last minute because he had too much revision to do. They were little things that wouldn't normally rile either of us but which now blew into flare-ups that had us both saying nasty things about each other which we didn't honestly mean.

These tiffs had quite knocked the stuffing out of me. I hate arguing, so to feel I was being treated like a verbal punchbag at times had dragged me down, both mentally and physically. I was beginning to feel really run down, though I wasn't sure whether that was a symptom or the cause of my stressed-out reactions to his niggling.

We'd seen less of each other than usual in the last month or so, but I knew how important his grades were, and I was happy for "us" to take a back seat for a while. If I was being honest with myself, I was also grateful for the break, and more than happy to spend the odd Friday or Saturday night chilling out at home.

When we did get together I tried to make allowances for him when he snapped or blew a fuse with me. I knew I had to be as supportive as my often frayed temper would allow, as I was acutely aware that this time next year I would be in the same situation, and crikey only knew how *I* was going to handle the pressure of exams.

I was brought back to reality by the sudden movement of Tim's arm next to mine as he leant forward to pick up the remote and turn the television off.

"Look, Luce," he said gently, turning to look at me with intense eyes, "we have to talk. There's something I've been meaning to tell you."

His tone of voice was unlike anything I'd heard before, and it worried me. My brow automatically furrowed and I stared at him, concerned.

"What? What's wrong?" I demanded.

"I . . . er . . . um . . . I don't quite know where to start." He scratched his chin in the way that he always does when he's nervous or about to make a suggestion he knows I won't like, like watching footy on the television rather than *Brookside*.

Then I noticed that his hands were shaking and I suddenly felt sick in the pit of my stomach.

It was then that I knew he was going to say something awful.

"There's someone else. . ." His voice trailed off and he looked away from me and fixed his eyes on some distant, neutral, point in the room.

"Wh–what?" My brain didn't quite understand what he was saying, the warning bells ringing in my head drowning out any ability to comprehend his words.

"I've met someone else," he said, as though trying to qualify himself. Then he added, "I'm so sorry. . ." He faltered again, but managed to drag his eyes back to mine so that I could see the fear etched on his face.

I couldn't take in what I was hearing. I suddenly had the surreal feeling that the scene I was experiencing was in fact a particularly unpleasant dream that I would soon wake up from.

I heard a voice speak. It was mine, although it didn't sound like me and I certainly wasn't aware of instructing it to say anything. "Who is she? Do I know her?" it said in a flat, matter-of-fact way.

"No," he replied. He opened his mouth as though he was going to add something else, then, deciding against it, shut it again.

Silence.

I felt my world collapse around me. I think I must have stopped breathing, because I heard myself gasp and a huge rush of oxygen blasted into my brain, making me feel light-headed and as though I might faint. What was he telling me? That it was over between us? He'd met someone else, someone to take my place?

"So we're . . . finished?" I said eventually, a note of incredulity in my voice.

"I still love you, Lucy. I'll always love you. But I'm. . ." he broke off again, looked away from me and whispered the few, fatal words that confirm the end of a relationship . . . "I'm not in love with you. I'm sorry."

I was outraged. He wasn't in love with me! How dare he not love me!

"Will you bloody well stop saying how sorry you are!" I seethed, anger overriding all other emotions. "It's pathetic! You're not sorry; how can you be? You're dumping me, for God's sake, because you're at it with another girl! How the hell can that make you *sorry*?"

I shot him a look of fury. I was humiliated beyond belief. I felt so stupid. I had no idea what had been going on. There I was, blindly believing that everything was all right between us – that he was even going to ask me to marry him – when in fact he was plotting his getaway all along.

"How long has it been going on?" I demanded.

"Not long. . . A month, maybe. . ."

"A month? You mean to say you've been two-timing me for a whole month? Why didn't you tell me before?"

"It never seemed to be the right time. I didn't want to hurt you. . ."

I snorted indignantly. "That's bull too. If you didn't want to hurt me you wouldn't be having an affair. You'll be telling me *(sarcastic voice)* 'It just happened' next. Like it was out of your control."

"Well, it *was* like that," he replied softly. "I didn't mean it to happen; I wasn't going out *looking* to meet someone else. I thought I was perfectly happy with you, that's the truth. This whole thing has totally bowled me over."

He looked down at his fingernails, then clasped his hands together to stop them from shaking.

"It's as much of a shock to me as it is to you," he added. "Please believe me when I say that, Luce."

From sitting in a bolt upright – uptight – position on the sofa, I sank back into the soft padded cushions, and felt waves of nausea begin to wash over me. All I could hear in my head were two words: *It's over.*

I was dumbfounded. I couldn't imagine anything more terrible ever happening to me. This had to be the ultimate low point in my life.

"*What* was a shock to you? What do you mean?" I said, unable to understand what he was saying.

"What I mean is that I never expected this to happen to me. It's like something you only ever see in the movies. When I met her it was instant; it really was love at first sight. We just connected. I can't explain it, it just felt right. It's like I didn't know what real love was until I met Amy, and the truth is that what I feel for her is different to what I feel for you. It's like my life has gone on to another level, one you and I would never have reached."

"But we were happy together," I said. "I don't understand what's changed."

"I've changed. And the way I feel about you has changed. I'm in love with her, that's all there is to it."

"And she's in love with you?" It was a rhetorical question. I just wanted to hear him kick me even harder in the stomach than he already had.

"Yes."

"So that's it then," I said resignedly. "The past two years have meant nothing to you."

"They've meant everything to me," he

implored. "Really they have. We've had some great times and I think you're a wonderful person. But we're not right for each other. I know that now. You deserve someone better than me."

"You're right there," I muttered bitterly. "Preferably someone who isn't a liar and a cheat."

"Believe me, I don't feel good about this," he replied, his voice wobbling slightly. "The last thing I ever wanted to do was hurt you; you have to believe me when I say that. I really thought we'd be together for the rest of our lives – you know, have a family together, grow old together. But then I met Amy. . ."

His voice trailed off and I felt my eyes fill with tears. *That's what I wanted too,* I thought bleakly. *A house and kids and our whole lives together. But it isn't going to happen. . .*

Not wanting him to see how much I was hurting inside, I fought back the tears and stood up.

"I have to go," I announced in a strained voice as I headed for the door.

"At least let me give you a lift home." He looked slightly surprised at my sudden decision to leave.

"No, really," I said, opening the front door and feeling an icy blast of cold air rush through my body. "I could do with the walk, sort my head out a bit."

"Come on, Luce," he implored. "It's freezing outside."

"I know. It's OK. Really." Didn't he see? I *wanted* to be outside in the cold. I wanted it to numb the pain I was feeling.

"I'll call you," he said. "Tomorrow. To make sure you're OK."

"No, don't," I said definitely. "I'll ring you sometime." I gave him a weak smile. "Goodbye, Tim."

Turning away, I walked out of the house and out of his life.

Chapter 2

I walked through the city towards home in a kind of stupefied daze, a relentless stream of hot, silent tears burning little rivulets into my frozen face. It was about nine-thirty on a Friday night and the streets were alive with merry people wandering from pub to bar to club, all getting into the Christmas spirit and smiling and saying hello to passers-by they'd normally pretend not to see. Jolly Father Christmases beamed out from shop windows and prettily coloured fairy lights winked on and off from every angle.

I stumbled along, not wanting to catch anyone's eye in the state I was in, feeling oddly alone in a world united in joviality and goodwill.

A bitter wind cut through my clothes and wrapped itself around me like an icy blanket, adding to the chill and rawness of the air which, as expected, I found strangely comforting.

I could hardly take the devastating news in. It was a huge shock to me. How could I have been so stupid as not to have realized that something was up between Tim and me? And to think that less than an hour ago I'd been harbouring the dumb idea that he was going to propose! Deluded or what? Had I been so completely besotted that I'd been viewing our relationship through rose-tinted glasses? Was my outlook so blinkered that I didn't notice something – any little thing – was amiss? I know I'd been feeling a bit tired and fractious myself recently, but not so much that I wouldn't notice my boyfriend of two years was no longer interested in me, surely?

Endless questions were whizzing around my head. I was so confused. It felt as though my heart had been ripped out and trampled on, then flattened completely by a giant steamroller. I felt utterly desolate and alone, empty of all feelings.

Images of Tim and Amy together kept flashing through my head, and although I didn't know what she looked like, I imagined her to be devastatingly attractive, much more so than I would ever be. Was she blonde, I wondered, like me? Or a dusky brunette of the type Tim sometimes admitted to fancying from afar? Was she more fashionable than me, brighter, more fun, better company, slimmer?

I cursed myself for not sticking to the diet I'd begun a few weeks back. It had lasted precisely two days, and was only one of a lifetime's worth of failed attempts to rid myself of my flabby stomach and thunder thighs. At five feet ten I was tall enough and large-framed enough to hide a multitude of sins under the baggy shirts and loose clothes I usually wore, but if I was being honest with myself I knew I could do with losing a few pounds. Tim had never once referred to my size, which I thought was nice; and it was only my paranoia that made me see it as a possible reason for his infidelity now, not something based on factual evidence.

My mind started to build up a picture of them together, kissing, laughing, Tim having the best time, or at least a much better time than he ever did with me. God, it hurt!

I racked my brain for clues as to his infidelity. There had been several occasions recently when I'd invited him somewhere – to the cinema, out with friends, bowling – and he'd declined, saying he had to study. It was obvious to me now that he was lying. He must have been with her.

Apart from that, there was nothing I could think of, no slip-ups in conversation, no time when he'd called me Amy by mistake or anything equally ridiculous.

I figured he must have been very clever to deceive me like that. It sounds dramatic to say he was leading a double life, but that was the stark reality. Even if it had only lasted a month or so – assuming he was telling the truth, and I wasn't even sure of that any more – he had to be pretty cunning to get away with it. And damned dishonest to do it in the first place.

How could he be so underhand? After two years together, how could he do this to me? It crucified me to think I obviously meant so little to him that he could find it easy to cheat on me. Perhaps this was all my fault. Had I forced him into her arms, somehow, by being too clingy? Too demanding? Too boring? Too miserable? I knew I'd been feeling a little sorry for myself recently; I'd had a bug that I couldn't shake off and which was sapping all my energy, and I was suddenly aware that perhaps I'd been a bit moany and difficult to please in his company. Was that enough to make him go off me? Or maybe he'd been telling the truth when he said falling for her like that had been a complete shock to him.

As though she'd come along and swept him off his feet.

Oh, why did he ever have to meet her? We'd have carried on being happy together if it wasn't for her – he'd practically said that himself. It felt like he'd been stolen from me, whipped away from under my nose never to be seen again. And I was powerless to do anything about it. I kept thinking *I don't want it to end. I'm not ready. It's not my decision.*

I couldn't imagine not having Tim around. I felt panic set in, the sort of feeling you get when you first walk into a room at a party and you're on your own and don't know where to stand, who to talk to, what to do with your hands. I hadn't felt like that for over two years. I'd always had Tim by my side, supporting me. We were a couple. If one was invited somewhere, it was always assumed the other would come along too. We went everywhere together, did everything together. The thought of being on my own again terrified me.

The house was empty when I got home. Shona was out with her boyfriend and Dad was either working or in the pub, I had no idea which. I was glad not to have to talk to anyone, as I had a tear-stained face and a filthy headache. I desperately wished I could disconnect my brain from the rest of my body so that I could have a rest from the mental torture it was putting me through. So many questions were left unanswered, banging away incessantly inside my head, but with no clear cut answers.

I had an insatiable desire to find out more about this Amy person, my wretched replacement. I wanted to know where she lived, what her voice sounded like, what she did to pass the time when she wasn't stealing other girls' boyfriends. Even though I knew nothing about her, I felt I already hated her. Likewise, I found it marginally easier to cope if I held her entirely responsible for the demise of my relationship with Tim. Logic had been temporarily banished from my emotions.

I fleetingly harboured the illusion that maybe he was the innocent party in this terrible situation, that she'd somehow seduced him, casting a spell on him, enticing him into her evil clutches. I wondered if she got a kick out of having illicit affairs. Then I wondered if she didn't know of my existence, just as until a few hours ago I knew nothing of hers. For all I knew Tim might never have mentioned me to her. He could just as easily have led her to believe he was a free agent when she first chatted him up, or he chatted her up.

I wondered how they had met, under what circumstances, who made the first move, what was said. I wished I could have been a fly on the wall when they first laid eyes on each other, so that I could witness the amazing chemistry that — according to him — went on between them both. I wanted to watch them kiss, so that I could see if he kissed her like he did me, looked at her the same way that he'd looked at me a thousand times in our life together. In the way that he would look at me no more.

I began to cry again, distraught at the loss I was feeling, drained beyond belief. I sat on my bed and used the duvet as a hanky to soak up the overflow from my eyes and nose. I never realized it was possible to cry so much. The way I felt now, I wouldn't have been surprised if I shed tears over Tim for the rest of my life. I would never meet anyone to replace him, never again would I experience such a depth of emotion for someone. Life without him would surely be unbearable.

I couldn't let it end like this, where I simply walked out of his life and never saw him again. He meant too much to me. What if, say, three months down the line, he realized that this thing he had with Amy was a mistake? What would he do then? Try and get me back? Would I go to him? Of course I would. Like a shot.

I wondered if he knew this, or if I'd made such a hash of our parting tonight that he was left with the impression I loathed him and didn't want to have anything else to do with him. I badly regretted blowing up at him. I don't think I'd ever raised my voice to him like that before. But then, I don't think I'd ever been so angry, or shocked or humiliated before.

I shouldn't have done it though, not if there was the inkling of a chance that we might get back together once his fling with Amy was over.

I felt the slightest glimmer of optimism. Perhaps there was hope for Tim and me after all. He might have deluded himself into thinking he was in love with someone else, but she could be stringing him along. How was he to know if she wasn't? After all, they'd only known each other for a month or so. You can't honestly say you know someone well after such a short length of time. She might be the type to fall in and out of love with each bat of an alluring eyelid for all he knew. He could be just one foolhardy guy in a long line of meaningless affairs. I was confident that there was no way he could have the same depth of relationship with her after four weeks as he'd had with me over two years. Surely that counted in my favour.

A desperate, clinging hope cheered my mood slightly as I crawled under the tear-stained duvet. I wasn't ready to give up on Tim yet; I wanted him back and I felt quite determined to get him, whatever it took.

I slept heavily and for too long, so that when I eventually woke up at midday, I felt woolly-headed and groggy. I dragged myself into a sitting position and swung my legs out of bed, catching a look at myself in the full-length mirror on the wardrobe as I did so.

I looked hideous. My eyes were red and puffy from crying, the delicate skin around them so swollen I looked like I'd just done ten rounds in a boxing ring. Smudged mascara and dark grey eye pencil added to the beat-up look. I had a "bedhead" hairdo which you wouldn't believe was possible considering my blonde hair is cropped short. One side of my head was flattened, while the other was set in a kind of crop-circle swirl above my ear. And I could feel a bald patch at the crown of my head. My fair skin was blotchy and greasy and an unwelcome family of spots had taken up residence on my chin. To top it all I felt like I was going to throw up at any minute.

I lay back on the bed and waited for the

nausea to subside, regretting the fact that I hadn't eaten anything sensible yesterday – just a bag of chips and a Snickers bar – and vowing to improve my eating habits and get healthy again so I didn't keep waking up feeling so ill like I had recently. I wondered whether I ought to make an appointment to see the doctor. This bug I was suffering from had been dragging me down for so long I was beginning to forget what it was like to feel normal.

The resolution I'd made to myself about winning Tim back loomed in the nether regions of my mind, and I tried to push it back even further, determined not to let my thoughts run riot as they had last night. That only depressed me, and I needed to keep a sense of optimism here in order to carry out my plan of action (not that I had one yet).

The smell of toast wafted up the stairs and I managed to drag myself out of bed to investigate, the earlier waves of sickness being replaced by a furiously rumbling stomach.

A cup of tea wouldn't go amiss either, I decided as I made my way to the kitchen. As I expected it was Shona who was knocking up a plate of poached eggs on toast for herself. Not surprisingly, she looked a little nonplussed at the sight of the gruesome creature walking in on her.

"You look rough," she said bluntly. "Have you been in a fight?"

I grunted something incoherent (even to me) and nabbed a piece of toast from her plate.

"Gerroff!" she squawked, grabbing it back and holding the plate to her chest covetously, "Make your own, you lazy cow!"

I huffed dramatically, took two slices of bread from the bread bin and slid them into the toaster. Then I flicked the kettle switch on, sat at the table and glowered at my sister who came and sat opposite me.

Shona and I get on OK, probably better than a lot of sisters. We bicker, we've even come to blows occasionally, but we don't hate each other's guts like a lot of people seem to. She's nearly four years older than me and therefore a bit of a bossy boots. Ever since our mum walked out on us when I was eight, Shona's tried to act like the mother we don't have, which can sometimes be a bit hard to take when there's such a small age gap. She does all the food shopping and a lot of the cooking and sorts out the housework rota and regularly snitches about me to Dad, which would be really irritating except that he doesn't usually take any notice.

I suspect we'll get along a lot better once one – or both – of us has left home. Until then, we tolerate each other quite well but don't share big secrets like best friends or even some sisters do. And I couldn't ever imagine us talking about stuff like sex or periods in a million years.

Today I could tell by her voice that she was in a grumpy and/or hungover mood.

"So who won?" she continued. "You or Mike Tyson?"

"Ha-ha, very funny," I replied sarcastically. "You don't look so good yourself. What time were you out until last night?"

"Four o'clock. Me and Ryan went to that new club on Hooper Street. It was brilliant, really wild. We saw Tim there. Have you two had a bust-up or something?"

My head jerked up and my alarmed eyes met hers.

What was he doing out having a good time so soon after dumping me? More to the point, who was he with? I tried to stay calm.

"Why do you say that?" I said, answering her question with one of my own.

Seeing the obvious dismay on my face, Shona's tone changed from one of taking the mickey to that of the concerned parent. She patted my hand across the table before carrying on. "Because, Luce," she said, "if you haven't been in a fight then you've been blubbing, and for quite some time, I'd say. Am I right?"

I nodded solemnly.

"Wanna talk about it?"

"Not really," I said defensively. "There's not much to say. We had a fight and I walked out on him. But we'll sort something out, I'm sure. He must have gone out after I left his house. Who was he there with? Anyone you knew?"

Shona looked down at the floor and began twiddling with a few loose strands of long golden hair that had fallen in front of her eyes. My suspicions were immediately aroused. I hadn't known her for seventeen years without realizing when she was under pressure. And believe me, she was sweating right now.

"He was with some girl," she replied in that no-nonsense manner of hers.

"What do you mean?" I retorted.

Of course I knew damn well what she meant, and I was 99.9 per cent certain that she was talking about this Amy person, but for some masochistic reason I wanted her to spell it out to me. You know, kick a dog while it's down (is that how the saying goes?). And at least I knew I could rely on Shona to give me an honest answer to a question. She never failed to tell it like it was, even if you didn't really want to hear what she was going to say.

"I mean just what I said," she explained. "He was with someone. And I don't know who she was, but judging by the way they were acting with each other, it was obvious they were more than just good friends."

"What did she look like?" I couldn't stop myself from saying it, even though I knew it came out sounding desperate. But I *was* desperate. I wanted to know everything about her, so that I could work out what she had that I obviously didn't. Shona gave me a quizzical look as though I was asking her the oddest question in the world.

"We-ell," she mused, "she looked a bit gorgeous, all curly haired and pouty mouthed and skinny. Seriously. Even Ryan said so. That is, he did once he'd put his eyes back into their sockets. So how long has he been two-timing you?" she added abruptly.

Oh no! This was even more terrible than I thought. How could I compete against someone so stunning? Compared to me, who was tall and chunky with a pot belly and passion for chips and mayonnaise? It was impossible. I was in a no-win situation. No wonder he'd dumped me! It must be like trading in your Lada for a BMW.

Shona must have noted the stunned look on my face.

"I take it that's what you two fought over," she continued. "I mean, I'm not telling you anything you didn't already know here, am I?"

"No," I said, shaking my head. "Actually, he's dumped me for her. But I managed to convince myself that maybe it would be all right, that she'd get bored of him, or he'd tire of her, and we'd get back together. . ." My voice trailed off. *Though if she looks like how Shona says, I don't fancy my chances much,* I thought ruefully.

"No, it never works like that," Shona said emphatically. "In my experience, once you've split up with someone, there's never any point in going back out with them. It doesn't gel any more. There's usually some big reason why you've split in the first place – like one of you has been unfaithful – and you'll never get that trust back again, so there's no point in hankering after a reconciliation. That's what I think anyway, for what it's worth."

"Cheers," I said woefully. "Thanks for the vote of confidence."

"I'm not deliberately trying to put you on a downer, it's simply a fact of life," Shona continued in her *Dear Deirdre* way. "Think about what would happen if you and Tim did get back together, knowing what you know now. You'd have to be super-human not to let it bug you whenever you let him out of your sight. You'd be eaten up with jealousy wondering what he's up to, or who he might be chatting up when he's not with you. Even if you managed to stop yourself from coming right out and grilling him every time you saw him, you'd be thinking about it, worrying that he was up to something, and it would be bound to get in the way of your relationship. Honestly, Luce, you're better off putting it all behind you and getting on with your life."

Of course, while I didn't want to agree with what she was saying, my sensible sister was absolutely right. And yet here I was, clinging on to the broken boughs of a relationship which, frankly, had withered up and died as soon as Tim told me about his infidelity last night. It wouldn't really matter if my replacement looked like Quasimodo and had the personality of a Conservative MP, the fact that he'd chosen her over me should be enough to bring this episode of my life to an end.

I was kidding myself thinking Tim and I could carry on as though nothing had happened. I don't consider myself to be a particularly jealous person, but even I had sometimes felt a twang of insecurity on the odd occasion when his in-bred babe radar homed in on some stunning girl or other and his jaw dropped to the floor at the

33

same time as an excess of testosterone began pumping wildly around his body. Who wouldn't? The fact that I would tell him in an overly loud voice to put his tongue away, usually curtailed the frequency of such occurrences. It was only because I was so secure in my relationship with Tim that I was able to make light of a potentially argument-inducing situation. Would I feel so unthreatened in the future (assuming there was indeed a future)? I doubted it.

Shona stood up and continued making her breakfast. She'd given me her lecture and, as far as she was concerned, the subject was closed. Much as I hated to admit it, she often talked a lot of sense. Plus of course she'd had four more years of life on this confusing planet than me. She'd had her fair share of boyfriends and relationships – at least three in the past year alone – compared to me who'd only ever been out with Tim. What did *I* know about love and life and stuff? I had so little experience of it all, no wonder I was floundering around not knowing what to do or say for the best.

Though I probably wouldn't admit it to her face, I was grateful for my sister's interference. I was finally beginning to make sense of the horrible situation I was in. There was no future for me and Tim; how could there be? *He* loved someone else; *I* would never have the confidence to trust him again, so what was the point in trying to hang on to something that wasn't there any more? I had to let go, however much it hurt me to do so.

Chapter 3

I spent the rest of the weekend holed up in my bedroom, playing my most depressing CDs and crying a lot. I might have accepted the fact that my two-year relationship with the guy I thought was the love of my life was over, and that I had to move on, but it didn't stop me from bursting into tears of self pity every time I thought about "us", which was just about every passing moment. I dreaded going back to school on Monday. By then word would have got out about Tim and me splitting up, and I wasn't looking forward to being the source of various behind-the-hand whispering sessions, nor of keeping up the pretence of telling everyone through gritted teeth that I was "fine, no really, I'm over it", then disappearing into the loo to howl my head off.

Even worse was the knowledge that sooner or later I would bump into Tim. And I knew that would hurt. I couldn't stop loving someone overnight, my emotions didn't work like that. I wished that I could hate him for what he'd done to me; I wished I could stamp my feet and shout and fly into a rage at the very mention of his name. But I couldn't. Maybe that would come later; at the moment I just felt . . . empty.

At various points during the weekend Shona shouted up to me from the bottom of the stairs, asking if I wanted a coffee, lunch or a sandwich. My muffled grunts from within the confines of my room were rightly interpreted as a "no" to each enquiry, and she would wisely retreat for a few more hours, leaving me to wallow in my misery.

Dad had obviously been filled in on the situation because he gave me a really wide berth. Usually on a weekend he'd be hassling me to get out of my "pit" if I wasn't up and about by mid-morning. He hated the thought of any of us wasting half the day in bed, saying we ought to be out in the fresh air, no doubt cleaning the car or mowing the lawn or something equally unpleasant. On this particular weekend though he left me alone, unable to cope with the teenage trauma his youngest daughter was going through.

Dad's great at sorting out practical problems, like helping me devise a workable revision schedule for exams, or stopping my CD player from jamming whenever it gets to the third track on my Verve album. But when it comes to personal, "girl" stuff, he's useless. If it had been left to Dad, Shona and I *still* wouldn't know how babies were made, and he's the only person I know who goes all pink and embarrassed and starts clearing his throat when there's a love scene on the telly. You can hardly blame him. At fifty-three he's quite old for a dad, and he can be quite Victorian in his values and attitudes. And of course it doesn't help not having a mum around to shoulder some of the responsibility of bringing up kids, in particular girls.

I always assume mums are the sort of people a lot of girls go to when they've been dumped on the scrap heap of their love lives; but Shona and I wouldn't know. We've had no contact with ours since that fateful day eight years ago when she walked out on the family to live in Spain with another man. Poor Dad couldn't have known what he was letting himself in for when he took on the responsibility of bringing up two soon-to-be hormonally strung-out children. No wonder he worked all the time. It kept him out of our way.

I sometimes wondered how Mum could just up and leave the family she had helped nurture for so many years. Whenever we asked Dad why he said it was because she wanted her life back; that she didn't want to be just a mum and a wife any more, she wanted to be her own person. He was always very fair about her, I thought. He seemed to lack any bitterness towards her, which I found surprising as she'd left us in our grotty council house for this older guy who happened to be loaded. I think Shona and I resented her more than Dad did. How could anyone dump the kids they'd created for some old bloke with a villa in Spain? She'd done it out of pure selfishness, if you asked me.

And now, for only the second time in my life, I was being abandoned. And what a time for Tim to choose! There's never a good time to get dumped, but Christmas must be the cruellest and the worst. And here I was, with a good six or seven parties to go to. All with Tim.

It must be a huge dilemma for all couples who've just split up. You're so used to getting invited to places together, like you're one person, then suddenly you're ripped in half and left wondering what to do about all those joint invites you're not prepared to share any more.

The most sensible solution would probably be

for the girl to go to any dos her friends have organized, and the boy to go to any his friends have organized. Which is fine until you get to the invites from friends you've made since you became a couple. What then? That was my dilemma. So what do I do? Go anyway, on my own? The thought made me feel ill. Even if I did, imagine how awful it would be if I went and saw Tim and Amy there. Together. Snogging and stuff. Ugh!

The alternative was to stay in my bedroom for the entire festive season, becoming even more morose. That sounded like a much easier option.

I guessed it would help if I had a bunch of girl-friends I could call up, you know, to see if they were going to the parties. Then I could tag along and take comfort in the fact that I had some kind of moral support if I did happen to bump into my ex. Plus it would mean I had a group of people I could arrive and leave with, thus cutting out the awful feeling you get in the pit of your stomach when you arrive at a party alone and aren't sure if there'll be anyone inside that you know.

But I didn't feel like I had any girlfriends I could call up out of the blue. Stupidly, I'd let most of my friends drift away since I got involved with Tim. I stopped returning their calls, preferring to spend all my time with the guy I thought I was going to be with for the rest of my life. What a big mistake that was! Tim and I had spent so much of our lives together. We'd meet up and walk to school together. We'd meet at lunchtime. Then we'd rendezvous at the school gates at the end of the day, and walk home together.

The kids I shared classes with were great. We got along fine on one level, but they'd long since stopped asking if I wanted to join them at lunch, or go to the cinema or to a pub of an evening. I guess people only take so many "no thank yous" before they give up and let you get on with your life.

Until I'd met Tim I'd always hung out with Zoë, who I'd known since we found ourselves in the same form class at senior school. We soon became best friends and still were right up until she met Matt and – within a couple of weeks – I'd met Tim. That was when we drifted apart really. I think she felt the same way as me: our respective boyfriends were more important to us than our friendship. Zoë and Matt had got engaged a few months ago, so at least her story might have a happy ending.

My thoughts turned to Tim's Christmas present, which I'd spent months looking for and which was beautifully wrapped and sitting under our Christmas tree waiting for him to open on

Christmas Day. What was I supposed to do with it now? Give it to him anyway? I don't think so. Offer to sell it to him, at a profit? Not a bad idea. Or let it fester at the back of my wardrobe until it was forgotten about? The most likely answer.

For the umpteenth time I replayed Friday night's final scene between Tim and myself in my head, where I'd foolishly been day-dreaming about him presenting me with an engagement ring on the 25th, and began crying again. Big globules of salty wetness poured down my cheeks and dripped off the end of my nose. God, I was a mess! How could I be expected to do anything that involved being with other people for any length of time in this state of emotional turmoil, when I felt like I was on the verge of tears all the time? I dreaded going back to school.

I heard Shona's voice shouting at me from the foot of the stairs. There was a phonecall for me. I didn't need to ask who it was – virtually the only person ever to call me at home was Tim. I debated with myself whether to speak to him. I wasn't sure if I could handle talking to him without crying again. On the other hand, we did have some things to sort out, which I would prefer to do in private rather than in one of the very public corridors at school sometime.

I slouched out of my room and headed down the stairs to the telephone in the hallway. As I got nearer the bottom I had an idea. I forced myself to put a bounce in my stride and a note of joviality in my voice. I wasn't going to let him sense how devastated I was, no way. *Let him think I'm over him*, I thought. *Let him think he meant nothing to me.*

"Hello," I said reasonably brightly.

"Luce, it's Tim—"

"Oh, *hi*!" I replied in a voice meant to sound like I was surprised it was him. "What can I do for you?"

"I just called to see how you are," he said. "After Friday, I mean. I thought you might have phoned or called round." He sounded nervous, like he wasn't sure what my reaction was going to be.

"Why would I want to do that?" I breezed. "Anyway, I'm absolutely fine. How about you?"

"I'm OK. I . . . er . . . I felt like we parted on a bad note. I didn't want it to end like that. Everything I wanted to say came out wrong. I wanted to explain a bit more, put you fully in the picture."

"There's no need, really, Tim," I continued. "You made yourself perfectly clear. I don't need anything else explained. Now, do you want to arrange to come over some time and sort out your CDs and stuff from mine?"

I sounded so calm, so matter-of-fact, I was surpassing myself.

"Er . . . um . . . yeah, sure. Look, that isn't why I rang."

"No, no, of course not. But we might as well sort a few things out rather than leave it all hanging in mid air. Actually, if you trust me, I could sort your stuff into a box and drop it round to your house, leave it in the garage or something."

"Of course I trust you. . ." there was confusion in his voice. "Whatever . . . whatever suits you."

"OK. Oh, the other thing I wanted to sort out was what you intended doing about all these Christmas parties we've been invited to. Will you be going? I just don't think it would be a good idea if we both go – or even all three of us, if you see what I mean. It could be embarrassing for other people." It sounded bitchy, I know, but I couldn't help myself.

There was a good five seconds' silence on the end of the line. It was obvious I'd completely wrong-footed him. He was probably expecting me to beg him to come back. Or slam the phone down on him in a dramatic manner.

My super-cool exterior was a total shock to him.

"Um . . . right," he finally replied. "Well, I don't think I'll be up to going to any myself, so you carry on, you know, have a good time."

"Don't worry, I will. Well, unless there's anything else you wanted to discuss. . .?" I paused dramatically. I felt like I was having a high-powered business meeting over the phone, finalizing some multi-million-pound deal.

Tim coughed nervously. "No, I don't think so. I think we've covered everything. I'm glad you're OK. . ."

"Of course. Look, I must go. There's someone at the door. Thanks for calling. I'll see you around some time."

"See you, Lucy. Take care of yourself."

I put the phone down and dissolved into tears once more.

Chapter 4

The tears flowed even more freely and frequently after that. At first I was usually set off just by the very thought of Tim, but more latterly things like a photograph of us together, discovered down the back of the bed while giving my room its annual clean, did the trick. Or once when I was in the dentist's waiting-room and sat next to a guy who wore the same aftershave as Tim.

Ridiculous things had me running for the Kleenex. Like the theme tune to *Match of the Day* which was on telly on a Saturday night, and which at one time I used to hate. But now it carried a certain nostalgia that made me blub into one of the sofa "comfort" cushions which seemed to permanently nestle on my lap.

While I often felt like it, I never once cried in

front of Tim. I couldn't after all the bravado I'd given him on the telephone after he dumped me. Typically though, I seemed to be forever bumping into him around school, and while we would always acknowledge each other's presence, that was about it. For my part it felt like there was nothing left to say.

As I had expected we were the subject of some good pre-Christmas gossip, but then a rogue ex-student set fire to the Humanities department and Tim and I were suddenly yesterday's news.

The party season passed me by; I didn't have the guts or the energy to go out on my own, and declined Shona's offer of spending Christmas and New Year's Eve with her and Ryan at some dodgy night-club or other. Although it was nice of her to suggest it, I wasn't keen on playing gooseberry and pretending to enjoy myself when really I just wanted to be left alone. I still felt knackered all the time (another reason for giving the endless stream of festivities a miss). I had been suffering from stomach cramps for a while, and had been seriously tetchy as well, though I wasn't sure how much of that was due to PMT or the fact that I felt like my whole life was heading up a street marked "Dead End".

I finally stopped crying over Tim two months after we broke up. I was lying in bed one night when I realized that, for the first time since we split up, I hadn't blubbed at all that day. It was as if I had finally run out of tears.

Not long after, I met David.

I hadn't intended meeting anyone else. As far as I was concerned guys caused nothing but heartache, and I had already vowed to myself that I would never date again. It was the only way I could guarantee that I wouldn't get hurt.

So when I was slobbing around at home one Friday evening and the doorbell rang, the last thing I expected to see when I opened the door was an absolutely gorgeous specimen of hunkiness standing on the front doorstep. He was with Ryan, Shona's boyfriend.

Apparently Shona had called Ryan to say she was going to be late home from work, and as they were going to a place called the Comedy Club on this side of town, did he want to come to our house and wait for her?

Naturally, if I had known any of this, and if I had known that he was going to be bringing along his tasty mate, then I would have hidden in my room until they went away (not that I was being anti-social or anything). Or, in the hope that I might look a little more slinky in his presence, I would have stuck to the miracle diet I'd started last week when I realized I couldn't get into my chinos any more, but which I had abandoned yesterday after a mental tussle over a packet of Doritos.

As it was, I was caught out, looking a dreadful sight in tracksuit bottoms so old the bum and knees were virtually hanging out, and a shapeless sweatshirt with a big tomato sauce stain down the front from the cheese on toast I'd scoffed for lunch.

I blushed furiously at the sight of them both standing on the doorstep, smartly dressed for a night on the town and – in the friend's case – looking drop-dead gorgeous.

After Ryan had explained all the stuff Shona hadn't bothered to let me know about, I stood aside and let them both in.

"This is David," Ryan said by way of introduction as he breezed towards the living-room.

"Hi," said David, smiling as he brushed past me and followed his friend.

I stood in the hallway for a moment, not sure what to do. My instinct was to make a run for the stairs and disappear to my room, but I knew it would be impolite to leave them stranded in the living-room without going in and offering them a drink and having a conversation with them.

I was tempted to whizz upstairs and change into something slightly less dishevelled, but that would look obvious and I couldn't rely on Ryan not to come out with some smartarse comment. In the end, I decided I couldn't look any worse than I did already, so I followed them in and stood at the doorway to the living-room, trying to hide behind the door so they wouldn't notice the state I was in.

"So how long did Shona say she'd be?" I asked Ryan.

"Not long," he replied from the chair he'd made himself at home in, adding, "Mind if I put the football on?"

"Er no, not at all," I lied. "Do you both want a drink or something?"

"Depends on what kind of 'or something' you're offering," Ryan shot back, winking at his mate. They both laughed, and I went an even deeper shade of crimson and wished I could be somewhere else. Seeing my humiliation, Ryan spoke again.

"Sorry, Luce, you walked into that one. A coffee would be great. Thanks."

I looked from Ryan to David, waiting for him to say if he wanted anything, and taking the opportunity to soak up his breath-taking features once more. He had the kind of face all lead singers of boy bands seem to have – you know, pretty-boy looks, with finely chiselled cheekbones and a perfectly straight nose and eyes that were innocent-looking yet sexy all at the same time. He had lips like pillows and perfect teeth and dark brown hair cut in that slightly floppy, foppish style that demanded he run his hands through it like he was in the process of having his photo taken for a magazine.

"Same for me, if it's no trouble," the perfectly plump lips announced, smiling at me. I shook myself back to the real world and, acutely aware that I had been staring at him, retreated into the hallway at great speed. *How embarrassing*, I thought as I escaped to the kitchen. I must have looked so obvious, gawping at him like that. What a moron!

I clattered around the room, grabbing at crockery in a state of high anxiety and excitement rolled into one. Dormant "boy-friendly" emotions which had been resolutely packed away two months previously began stirring inside of me, clawing their way to the surface, alarming me with their ferociousness.

I stared at my face in the mirror over the sink. My skin was shiny, my hair greasy, and I had a line of blue biro drawn from my lip to my chin where I'd been absent-mindedly sucking a pen while ringing which programmes I'd intended watching on the telly tonight. I rubbed my face in a tea-towel to get rid of the shine and the pen and threw a load of coffee things on to a tray, then carried it into the living-room as gracefully as possible, desperately hoping it wouldn't be obvious that my hands were shaking.

"Help yourselves," I said as casually as I could, and placed the tray in the middle of the carpet. I then retreated to a chair and hoped neither of them would spot the hole in the bum of my tracksuit bottoms.

The pair of them dived on the coffee and biscuits I'd laid out. I saw David put three heaped teaspoonfuls of sugar into his black coffee, then top it up with as much milk as he could squeeze in the mug. Then he dunked biscuit after biscuit into the liquid and munched and slurped away happily. If it had been anyone else I would have been thinking what a greedy pig he was, but as it was him – well, he could have eaten off the floor for all I cared.

"So what's this comedy club place you're going to?" I asked in an attempt to get some kind of conversation going.

"It's a new thing a friend of David's has set up, like a showcase for new acts to do some stand-up comedy," Ryan explained.

"I got offered free tickets so we thought we'd check it out," added David.

"Oh."

I couldn't think of anything else to say, so just sat there fiddling with the top of one of my socks and desperately trying not to stare at David as he sat watching the football on the telly.

"Are you up to anything this weekend?" Ryan finally asked me during a lull in the play.

"Um . . . n-nothing special," I replied with extreme embarrassment. I realized that it was really naff not to be able to reel off a list of trendy clubs and bars I was planning to party in, but my mind wasn't quick-thinking enough to come up with a lie, even though I now seemed like a social retard (which, at the moment I probably was).

"You should come to the Comedy Club some time," David announced. "I can get you a couple of tickets, if you're interested."

"Thanks, that would be great." I smiled at him. *Especially if you're going to be there*, I thought lecherously.

"You could have come tonight if I'd known, but I've only got the three tickets," he went on.

"Never mind. Thanks anyway," I said in my most laid-back voice, but wondering frantically if he was keen on me or just being friendly. I heard the front door open and Shona rushed in. She poked her head into the room, then disappeared back into the hallway.

"Sorry I'm late, guys," she shouted as she flew up the stairs. "Give me another five minutes and I'll be ready."

The boys carried on watching the football and I sat in my chair trying to steal glances in David's direction when I thought he wasn't looking. He really was seriously cute, someone I could definitely while away the hours day-dreaming about. I wondered if he had a girlfriend, and figured (hoped?) not, since he was going out on a Friday night on his own. Mind you, someone as divine as him wouldn't be short of admirers and ones, I suspected, who looked a darn sight more delicious than I did at the moment. Still, there was no harm in fantasizing. . . Which I did for the next few minutes. I imagined what it would be like to kiss those juicy lips, to run my fingers through that pop-star hair. . .

Conscious that I was staring again, I was almost relieved when my sister reappeared in the living-room and the three of them trooped towards the door.

"Thanks for the coffee, Luce," Ryan grinned as he left.

"Yeah, thanks," said David. "I'll let you know about those tickets." He winked at me as he walked past and I barely managed a squeaky farewell, so powerful was the thrill running through my body.

I spent the rest of the evening in a happier mood than I had done for months. OK, so realistically I knew that I didn't have a hope of landing a catch like David – it would have been like dating Ronan Keating – but the encounter did me oodles of good. It made me realize that moping around feeling sorry for myself was a complete waste of a life. I had spent far too long mourning the loss of Tim, and now was as good a time as any to put it behind me and get over him.

The following morning I scrubbed myself up and went shopping for a new-look me, heading for the city centre where all the best stores were. The city was heaving, the roads heavy with weekend traffic and the pavements overflowing with masses of pedestrians out for a good day spending their hard-earned cash.

As I meandered from one shop to another, it was difficult coming to terms with the fact that I was now looking at racks of size fourteen clothes, rather than size twelve, but even that gave me the determination to cut down on biscuits and get in shape as part of the new, improved me. I suddenly decided against buying clothes in a bigger size, as this was now Day

One of my new diet and exercise regime and I was sure they'd be hanging off me in a few weeks' time. Instead, new make-up and accessories were put to the top of my list of necessities and I headed for the big department store in the High Street.

I began wandering down the street, looking idly into windows and imagining how I might look in the outfits the super skinny mannequins were sporting. For the most part, the answer would be pretty hideous. I'd always had a bit of a weight problem, but in the past any excess had gone straight to my thighs. Now all of a sudden it was accumulating around my waist. I wondered if I might be pregnant. . .

Suddenly I heard a voice calling me.

"Hey, Lucy! Over here!"

I looked vaguely over to where the yell was coming from and saw Jane Bennett from my year at school waving frantically at me. I walked hesitantly over to where she was standing with a group of friends I vaguely knew. What on earth did she want? We'd hardly said more than hello to each other in our entire time at school together. She was in the ultra-trendy crowd and was, I always thought, far too hip to mix with such a normal person as me. So why would she suddenly be interested in speaking to me? And why now, when I had far more important things on my mind?

"Have you heard about Tim?" she urged, wide eyed.

"No," I replied, frowning. "I haven't seen him to speak to for ages. Why?"

"*Well.* Are you ready for this?" She paused for the maximum dramatic effect before adding, "He's only getting married."

My jaw dropped to the floor and my eyes popped with amazement. I was staggered.

"What?" I gasped.

"Yes. *Married.* They announced it at her birth-day party last night." She looked hard at me, taking in the full range of my shock.

"Whose party?" I demanded. "Who's he get-ting married to?"

"You *know*," she grinned, her eyes rolling skywards at the stupidity of my enquiry. "*Amy.* Works in the record shop in town. She's a friend of my sister's. Wild, isn't it? They can't have been going out for more than a few months. . ."

I was having difficulty taking the news in. It was hurtful enough to know that Tim was in love with the wretched Amy, my replacement, but to hear that they were getting married as well was just too much.

"Are you *sure*?" I quizzed. "It's not just a rumour—"

"No, I was there," Jane yabbered excitedly. "I saw it with my own eyes; heard it loud and clear over the speaker system. And later on in the evening I bumped into Amy in the loo. She said they were frantically saving up for a house and were hoping to get married at the end of next year. You mean he didn't tell you?" The question was asked in a voice of utter amazement, like she thought it was outrageous that my ex-boyfriend hadn't told me he was getting married to someone else.

"Er . . . no," I said, stumped for anything else to say. It would have been nice to hear it from him rather than some gobby girl I hardly knew who was only divulging the information so she could spread the news of my reaction around – with great exaggeration, no doubt.

"Oh boy!" Jane went on, "I'd be so angry if someone did that to me."

If she was looking for a response she wasn't going to get it.

"Oh well, thanks for letting me know," I smiled sweetly at her. "I'll go and buy them a congratulations card right away. See you around."

I turned away from the gaggle of girls, leaving them visibly disappointed that they hadn't had a reply worthy of school gossip, and continued walking down the street.

I wandered aimlessly, not knowing where I was going, engrossed in my thoughts. A rush of *whys* were whizzing through my brain. Why was Tim getting married? Why her and not me? Why did I have to hear it from a third party and not him? And why did it bug me so much? After all, it wasn't as though we had anything to do with each other any more.

News like this just dredged up a whole load of mixed-up emotions again. I guess the feeling uppermost in my mind was one of hurt, not that he didn't have the decency to tell me what he was about to do, but that he'd asked her to marry him and not me. My pride had been seriously dented. Knowing that Tim had chosen to spend the rest of his life with someone he'd only known for – what? – three months, rather than the person he'd been with for two years, cut me to the quick.

Pathetic though it might sound, deep down I knew I wouldn't feel this way if I'd met someone else, but even that had eluded me. Oh, I know there was David. But he was just a fantasy, someone I could dream about but not ever have any real chance of going out with. Anyway, he was way out of my league.

I also thought that although I'd managed to convince myself that I was over Tim, really I wasn't. Part of me still harboured the illusion that someday he would realize his mistake and come back to me. That last – pitiful – hope had just been snatched away from me.

Chapter 5

I felt like my life had turned into a big roller-coaster ride. One minute I was up, the next thrown back into a trough of despair. I felt physically and emotionally drained, and had done for as long as I could remember.

I felt like I needed to sit down, so I crossed the street and went into Burger King, where I ordered a coffee and took a window seat looking out on to the pavement with hordes of people buzzing around. I stared out at them, vaguely watching as they beetled up and down the street, like a parade of ants going about their highly important business.

My attention was caught by the sight of a girl walking across the main road in my direction. She was carrying a baby in one arm and a giant-sized bag of nappies plus a couple of carrier bags in the other. She looked even more glum than I imagined I must appear. The thing that struck me most about her was her age. I knew it was unlikely to be true, but she looked about twelve years old, certainly not old enough to be a mother. I wondered whether it was her own child, or whether she was looking after it for someone else. But she didn't seem to be with anyone else, and who in their right mind would entrust their baby to someone who was little more than a child herself? I assumed she was a young mum, and felt sorry for her, though I couldn't put my finger on any one reason why.

Suddenly, my thought processes backtracked to the unsettling notion I'd implanted in my brain about ten minutes ago, before the shocking news about Tim and Amy had come along and momentarily pushed it to the back of my mind. All of a sudden, like a thundering high-speed train, it came rumbling back and hit me right between the eyes.

I might be pregnant. I took my diary from my bag and began scanning the calendar at the front end of the book. I was trying to work out when my last period had been. Certainly not this year. I turned back a page to last year's calendar and studied it intently. It must have been around October time, certainly no later than November. We were now in the middle of February. So it could be as much as four months since I had had a period.

This wasn't so unusual. For a lot of people, I guess, missing a period would be a huge pointer to the possibility of being pregnant. But not for me. I didn't start my periods until I was fifteen, and they'd always been irregular, never having settled into any kind of pattern. It wasn't at all unusual for me to go three months or more without one, so I hadn't been unduly worried – it hadn't even crossed my mind that I might be late. I'd read in a magazine that it can sometimes take a few years before you get into any kind of monthly routine, if ever. And although being on the Pill while I was with Tim had settled them into a clockwork routine, I had stopped taking it when we split and had half-expected my cycle to be all over the place again.

There had been other previously unexplained episodes that didn't mean much individually, but which collectively added up to a really scary scenario. The fact that I had been feeling so grim in recent months should have sounded warning bells in my head. But didn't. It seemed obvious now that the nausea I sometimes felt when I woke up was morning sickness. And there I was, thinking it was because I hadn't been eating properly.

And what about the mystery bug I thought I'd been suffering from? The tiredness? The grumpiness? And, of course, I'd put on weight. Why on earth hadn't that spelt it out to me? Probably because I'd naïvely put it down to the fact that I'd been troughing more than my fair share of chocolates and sweets recently. I'd assumed I'd been comfort eating; some kind of short-lived consolation for the break up of my relationship with Tim. *Could* I possibly be pregnant? I wondered. Or was I scaring myself stupid unnecessarily? There was only one way to find out. I would have to take a pregnancy test.

Leaving my coffee untouched, I strode purposefully to the door. The sooner I got this over and done with, the better. Once outside, I made a left turn and headed for the large Boots a few doors away from where I'd been sitting. I was grateful that I was in the city's main shopping centre rather than one nearer home. At least this way I could be sure of a certain amount of anonymity when I needed it most. The last thing I wanted was to be spotted buying a pregnancy test by someone I knew.

Nevertheless, it still felt like all eyes were on me as I wandered up and down the aisles, as though everyone in there knew what I was looking for, and was watching my every furtive move. Of course, I had no idea where to find pregnancy tests, no notion of whether they were displayed on the shelves or kept under lock and key out the back somewhere. I'd never been in a position where I'd needed to buy one before. And although I'd seen adverts for them in magazines and on the television, I'd never really taken in how you used them or how they worked. It was a whole new experience for me.

After several trips around the store I finally spotted them lurking on a low shelf near the mineral supplements. My eyes swept people's faces on the shop floor before I dared pick one up, just in case. And when I did I felt like I had a sign above my head saying "Look at me" as I sauntered over to the check-out as blithely as I could manage. I glanced with some embarrassment at the woman on the till, but she kept her eyes averted from mine, her interest in my purchase completely non-existent. Still, I was enormously relieved when I managed to get out of the shop without being seen by anyone I knew.

Deciding that I couldn't wait until I got home to find out the result, I turned in the direction of Debenhams situated five minutes' walk away. I figured the public toilets on the fourth floor were as good a place as any to discover the truth. I hurried on, all the while the contents of my stomach and my brain churning nervously. I tried to banish my troubled thoughts from my mind – after all, there wasn't any point in worrying when I didn't yet know if there was anything to fret over. I tried to change the subject in my head, and turn my attention to something rather more pleasant. But I couldn't come up with anything. Everything else was obliterated.

I was relieved when I got to the store, and was able to stride to the escalator and make my way onwards and upwards towards my fate.

By the time I got to the Ladies I was tense with anticipation. I could hear my heart thumping against my chest as I walked into an empty cubicle and took the long, slim box out of my bag. My hands shook as I read the instructions six, maybe seven times, then I carried them out as precisely and accurately as I could.

I stood up from the loo and stared at the two windows in the white plastic test stick, waiting for the result. According to the instructions, a line was supposed to appear in the round window to show that I'd used the test properly. Then, if I was pregnant, a line would also appear in the square window. It was only supposed to take a minute, but it felt like an hour as I watched intently, my hand shaking all the more now, my breath held in anticipation.

Suddenly a line magicked itself into the round window as if from nowhere. Then, moments later, I watched goggle-eyed as a line appeared in the square window as well. I swallowed hard in an attempt to force my heart from my throat back down into my chest, and leant heavily against the toilet door for support. This was unreal! I read the instructions again and again, wondering if perhaps I'd got it wrong. But no. I had no reason to doubt the test. It was proven to be over ninety-nine per cent accurate, and it confirmed my worst fears. I was pregnant.

Although I'd been mulling the prospect over ever since I sat down in Burger King, it didn't lessen the shock one iota. I was absolutely stunned. *This can't be happening to me!* I thought. *Surely I'll wake up in a minute and realize this whole day has been a horrible dream?* But I knew that wasn't going to happen, I knew deep down that I'd been ignoring something that had been staring me in the face weeks ago.

My mind was racing. Pregnant? How the heck did I manage to get pregnant? Tim and I had never taken any chances; we'd always taken precautions. I'd been on the Pill, for heaven's sake! I didn't understand how this could possibly have happened.

What was Tim's reaction going to be when I told him he was going to become a father? If we were still together he'd be shocked, though I liked to think he'd be supportive too. But add to that the fact that we'd actually split up and he was not only in love with someone else, but engaged to be married to them . . . well, he'd be absolutely devastated. He was even more adamant than me about not wanting children before he was thirty. This news would crucify him.

What am I going to do? I thought. I can't bring up a child, I'm not ready for it. I didn't plan on having a baby for at least another ten years. More to the point, I don't *want* a baby now. I can't look after a child. I'm hardly capable of looking after myself, let alone another human being. The image of the young girl I'd seen with a baby just minutes ago came into my head again, only this time it was my face on her body, me looking miserable, fraught, and resigned to the loss of what should have been the most care-free years of my life.

There has to be a way out, I thought. Deep down I knew there was an escape route, one that

I had hoped I would never have to consider in my life. Now there didn't appear to be any alternative.

What about an abortion? I thought. It was difficult to believe I was sitting here contemplating getting rid of the baby I'd only just found out I was carrying. I'd sometimes asked myself if I would have an abortion if I ever fell pregnant by accident and, harsh as it may sound, for me there had only ever been one choice. I didn't want to be one of those gymslip mums you hear about on the television. I wanted to have a normal life before I started planning a family. Plus I'd always intended being in a stable relationship. And I'd always assumed that if I fell pregnant by accident I would at least have Tim around to help me get through it.

Now, standing here all alone and hearing myself ask the question in a real life situation, I wasn't so sure about the outcome. Could I really bring myself to get rid of the baby that was growing inside me? I was no longer so confident I would be able to go through with it. In fact, I was pretty convinced I couldn't.

I became aware that I must have been standing in this tiny loo for a good ten minutes, and it was beginning to feel rather oppressive in there. I gathered my things together, unlocked the door and went outside. I washed my hands automatically and had a quick look at myself in the mirror. I looked just the same as when I had walked in. Who would have thought that, when so much had changed in such a short time?

I felt unsteady on my feet as I walked back out into the fresh air. My body felt numb, while my brain went into an acceleration of thoughts and questions and conundrums. In the space of less than a minute my life had been turned upside-down once and for all. Nothing would ever be the same again. I couldn't even begin to contemplate quite how much of an effect this news was going to have on the rest of my years on this planet. It was too much to take in. What about school? My exams? My career? What would happen to all these things which I considered so important, but which had an increasingly bleak outlook?

And what about my dad? What would he think? I was panic stricken once more. I couldn't bear my father knowing about this. I could just imagine the scene if he found out. It takes a lot to get Dad riled but when he does both Shona and I pray that the other one is the cause of it. He can terrify both of us with a single word and a look.

I remembered the rollicking he gave Shona a

couple of years back when she was sick after drinking cider down at the shopping centre with a group of mates. She was brought home in a police car in a complete state of paralysis and threw up all over the front doorstep. She was grounded for a month and made to write a letter of apology to the local constabulary for wasting police time. That would pale into insignificance compared to the news that Dad's other daughter was seventeen and up the duff. I really believed he would kill me for that. He's always banging on about how important a good education is – in the form of degrees and Ph.D.s and stuff – in order to get on in life. And I was supposedly the most academically minded of the family with my eight GCSEs and in my first year of study for three A Levels. I guess he's got high expectations for me, aspirations which would be dashed as soon as he found out about me. No, Dad mustn't find out about the awful mess I was in. Not yet.

I made my way home, completely absorbed in my thoughts. I only knew of one girl from my school who'd become pregnant in similar circumstances. She was sixteen and had been studying for her exams, just like me. I remember her pregnancy was really big news at the time and the talk of the school corridors for months. People nudged each other and whispered behind their hands whenever she walked by; spiteful kids called her names and she suddenly developed a reputation for being easy, which was doubtless unfounded. In the end she was taken out of school and allowed to complete her studies with a private tutor. The story was that she went into labour during her geography exam, but I suspect that was just a rumour which was wildly exaggerated.

These days I sometimes see her at the city shopping centre, pushing a buggy and child round and round the mall, looking thirty-eight years old instead of eighteen. I feel sorry for her; well, you would, wouldn't you?

I didn't want that to happen to me. I didn't want to be the source of local scandal, made to feel like a piece of dirt for one dumb mistake. I suddenly came to the conclusion that no one must find out about this. So far no one had suspected I was pregnant, least of all me. If I could keep it to myself for a while longer I could buy some time and think about what I was going to do.

Chapter 6

As I made my way home I felt my head clear a little and I attempted to trace back to how I might have got pregnant. I racked my brain but I could think of nothing, no obvious mistakes Tim or I might have made with contraception – nothing, in retrospect, that might have led to *this*.

But, hang on a minute, there *was* something. I'd had really bad food poisoning several months ago. God, when was it? It must have been some time last September or October. I remembered being violently sick for days. I never gave it a thought at the time when I took my contraceptive pills, but now I wondered if they'd had a chance to work, or if I had unwittingly thrown one or more of them up beforehand? I bet that was what happened and that, I had, in effect, missed a pill and therefore been susceptible to falling pregnant. What a fool, what a stupid damn idiot! That had to be it; there was nothing else I could think of. What a dumb mistake!

If that was the case, then I must be quite far gone. I stopped in my tracks and took out my diary once more and counted up the weeks from the beginning of October to today. Twenty weeks or thereabouts. Twenty weeks out of a nine-month pregnancy. It seemed like an age. I wondered how big the baby would be at this stage. Would it have fingers and toes? What was it doing in there? I hadn't felt it moving around. Maybe it didn't do that until much later. My knowledge of such matters was practically non-existent. I'd always avoided getting into conversations with pregnant women, or aunts and uncles with young children. It seemed like they lived a life poles apart from mine and I couldn't relate to them at all. And yet here I was, about to become one of them, someone with the huge responsibility of a child, when previously the only responsibility I had was to feed my pet goldfish once a day. If it wasn't so frightening, it would be funny.

My thoughts turned back to Tim. How was I going to tell him? It would be almost as bad as telling my father. I tried to imagine what his reaction might be when I announced that he was soon to become a dad to the child of his ex (and long-forgotten) girlfriend. He'd certainly be stunned, as I was, but would he be prepared to become the rock of support I desperately needed to help me get through this? Would he accept that the baby growing inside me was as much his responsibility as it was mine?

Oh, if only I could be sure Tim's reaction was going to be positive! I thought as I trudged the streets towards home. If I could, I wouldn't have so many qualms about putting him in the picture, and I'd feel much more able to face up to my life from now on. But I knew my mind was playing tricks on me. Tim wasn't going to come back to me because of this. He wasn't going to give up Amy, his big love, for the girl he dumped just a few months ago. The much more likely scenario would be that he would (hopefully) accept responsibility for being the father, and offer to help support me as much as he could. He might even be interested in seeing his child in a part-time-father sort of way. But that's where it would end. That was the most likely outcome.

I wasn't even sure I was going to tell Tim at all. Why ruin his life as well as my own? What would be the point in that? If I did tell him, what's to say he wouldn't accuse me of getting pregnant deliberately in order to try to trap him into coming back to me. It would be totally out of character, but who knows what goes through a guy's mind when he's got his back to the wall and is faced with such an earth-shattering piece of information? I thought I would have done anything to get Tim back when he dumped me, but I wouldn't resort to that – no decent person would.

Whatever happened, the reality of it was that I was going to have to face my radically changing life on my own. The thought petrified me, tied my stomach in knots the size of tree trunks, and made me feel physically ill.

I contemplated walking right past my house and carrying on walking. For ever. As though if I carried on for long enough I would be able to leave the problems behind that were currently spiralling out of my control. But of course, I didn't. I went up the path and put the key in the lock and turned it, just as I did every other day, as though nothing had changed.

As I opened the door I could hear Shona rattling around in the kitchen preparing tea for the family. The thought of confiding in her flashed through my mind for a second or two.

Realistically, she was the only person I could turn to. I could rely on her to be supportive, as well as practical and sensible and mature and all the things I knew I wasn't.

I wandered into the kitchen and saw her huddled over the sink, peeling potatoes.

"Fancy a coffee?" I said as lightly as I could manage.

"Mmm, please," she replied, then swore as the knife she was using slipped and unintentionally chopped a big lump of potato from the chunk she was viciously attacking.

"You're home late," she went on. "Where have you been?"

I looked at her for a second, wondering whether it would be a good idea to launch straight into *Well, actually no. I went shopping. Oh, and by the way, I'm pregnant.* Then I thought better of it and chickened out.

"I got chatting to some people and lost track of time," I said, thinking quickly.

"You should have told me this morning. You know I hate it when you're not home when you say you will be."

I judged by her snappy reaction that she was obviously in a bad mood. Was it worth trying to have a heart-to-heart with her in her current frame of mind? I walked over to one of the eye-level cupboards and began rooting around inside, playing for time, trying to sort out in my mind what, if anything, I was going to say to her. I found a half-eaten packet of chocolate Bourbon biscuits and took a couple out, ready to eat with my coffee. Shona gave me a disapproving look from the sink.

"You could do with leaving those alone, Lucy. Have you looked at yourself in the mirror recently? You're getting really lardy."

Right, that was it! I slammed the biscuit packet down on the work surface and stormed out of the kitchen and up the stairs to my room.

Stuff her! I thought. The irritable cow! If she knew that the excess baggage around my waist was a baby, she'd soon shut up. Anyway, what was I doing thinking I could confide in her? Shona had always sneered at girls "stupid enough to get pregnant". They deserved no sympathy in her book. And anyway, she'd be bound to tell Dad – there was no way she'd be able to keep a secret like that to herself. Telling her was a dumb idea. The truth was, Shona was the second-to-last person I ought to tell (after Dad). I couldn't trust her to keep her mouth shut; I was mad to even contemplate confiding in her. But it made me realize how desperate I was to unburden myself. And the fact that I had no one to share this with made me despair even more.

I went to the bathroom and started to run a bath for myself. I removed my clothes and stood naked in front of the full-length mirror on the bathroom door. I studied my body from the front then stood to the side and peered at myself from that angle too. For the life of me, I didn't look how I expected a pregnant woman to look.

I'm quite a big person, tall and with what you would probably call a largish frame. My shoulders are bigger than a lot of girls my age, and my feet are a size seven, so we're not talking Kate Moss here. Even so, quite where a living, breathing, ever-growing baby was hiding, I could only guess at.

I scrutinized myself critically. My normally quite thick waist looked perhaps a little wider than usual, and from the side I had the makings of what I'd previously thought was a chocolate-filled paunch; nothing too excessive though. And I certainly didn't look like the pregnant women you see huffing their way around town on a Saturday afternoon, all waddling like ducks from the back and giving the impression they're carrying a small family car between their legs. I guessed that would come later.

I poked my tummy with my index finger in an attempt to provoke a reaction from the being slumbering inside. Nothing. I thought back to any odd feelings I might have experienced in the previous months. I *had* been suffering a lot from what I thought was indigestion recently. Maybe that was what a baby's kick felt like, not the Dr Marten's boot in the belly I'd always assumed it to be.

I walked closer to the mirror, wiped the film of steam from its surface and examined my face. Where was the glow expectant mums are supposed to emit from every pore, that aura of health and vitality that's reckoned to follow you around for nine months? I just looked wretched, with spots and a shiny pink face from the steam-filled room and blackheads on my nose.

Maybe the test had been wrong. It said on the leaflet that it was over ninety-nine per cent accurate. Maybe I was one of the remaining one per cent? It was a long shot and I knew I was clutching at straws, but it was the only door left open for me to flee through. And believe me, right now I was looking for any means of escape.

I stepped into the bath and lay down, letting the warm water and bubble bath wash over me. Maybe the only way to stop worrying about this was to block it from my memory, pretend it never happened. Perhaps if I could do that, if I could ignore it for long enough, then it would go away.

Chapter 7

Of course, it didn't go away. The bump seemed to explode overnight from what I'd previously thought was a pot belly to a humungous bulge. I felt like I was walking around with a sign on my head saying "Look at me! I'm pregnant!". This was, of course, an acute case of paranoia. In fact, the bump was no bigger, only in my imagination.

However, I'd decided that I was going to tell no one about the pregnancy, partly because I believed that the more people who knew the more likely it was to become common knowledge, but mostly because I felt that if I confided in anyone it would mean I would have to face up to what was happening to me, and I wasn't ready to do that just yet. So I virtually blanked everything from my mind and got on with my life as though nothing had happened.

I badly felt that I needed to see Tim. I couldn't explain why; perhaps deep down I felt – hoped? – that I could blurt everything out to him, to relieve some of the tremendous pressure I was under. I honestly didn't know.

However, determined to get the moment over and done with, I went back to school on the Monday and spent much of my time going out of my way to run into him accidentally. I loitered near his maths block during morning breaks, walked around the football pitch for most of my lunch breaks, and kept popping into the canteen at various times during the day. They were all places I knew he hung out and which I'd previously avoided as much as possible. But to no avail.

When I did see him it was in the very worst circumstances. It was towards the end of the week. I had a free afternoon for private study and as it was Shona's birthday soon and I hadn't yet bought her anything, I nipped into the city shopping centre for a couple of hours.

It was going to be her twenty-first birthday and so I wanted to get her something special, maybe a gold chain or a pair of gold earrings. I toiled around endless jewellery shops, peering in their windows, looking for something that was a reasonable price without looking cheap or tacky. I actually saw a lovely nine-carat gold chain at a reduced price in the first shop I went in, but, always one to hunt for a better bargain, thanked the sales assistant for showing it to me and carried on looking.

Two hours later, and having found nothing to match it, I went back to the first shop and, without hesitating, opened the door and walked straight in.

Straight into Tim. With Amy. At first they didn't see me. They were too engrossed in looking at a tray of rings. Amy was trying one on the third finger of her left hand and they were both admiring the way it sparkled. Tim had his arm around Amy's shoulder and he was looking into her eyes and smiling. He really did look like he was in love with her.

I stood in the open doorway, taking the scene in, momentarily transfixed on the spot. A draught from outside must have been blowing in on them because Tim turned his head in the direction of the doorway, a vaguely irritated look on his face as though he was thinking how rude it was of the person who'd just walked into the shop not to close the door behind them.

When he saw me his expression turned to a

mixture of astonishment and acute embarrassment.

"Er . . . hello Tim," I managed to say in a reasonably cheerful voice in spite of the total desolation I felt. Memories I'd purposely pushed to the far reaches of my mind came flooding back. There had been many a time when I had dreamed of the day that Tim and I would go shopping for an engagement ring, the seal of love I had so badly wanted. I never expected to see him buying one for someone else. Wasn't it ironic then that here I was, carrying inside me the ultimate gift of love two people can ever possess, but had no one to share it with!

Tim obviously read my upbeat tone (albeit fake) as some kind of approval of the moment I had unexpectedly walked in on, because his mouth broke into a broad grin and he came over to where I was rooted to the spot and gave me a big bear hug, the kind that guys give each other when they want to show their affection for their male chum, but at the same time they don't want any onlooker getting the idea that they might be, you know, *that* way inclined. It was all-enveloping and cosy yet meaningless, a hug that acknowledged I was there but which was not in any way sexual.

"Hello, Lucy! Great to see you," he grinned.

"Amy," he motioned over to his fiancée, who was still sporting the solitaire diamond and gold ring on her finger, "come and meet Lucy. *You* know. . ." The way he said "You know" and then trailed off was, I guessed, to avoid having to tack "my ex-girlfriend" on to the end of the sentence. I didn't know whether I was grateful for his diplomacy or angry that he wasn't acknowledging my status, but before I could think about it for too long, Amy was at his side, beaming at me, a great big banana of a smile that stretched right across her face. She wasn't at all how I had imagined (they never are, I thought dolefully). She was small and curvy, with a tiny waist and well-endowed chest. She had long dark curly hair, big lips, and a small button nose. Her eyes were almond shaped and green and looked rather like a cat's. She was undoubtedly attractive, but not the drop-dead stunner I'd expected at all.

"Hello," she said. "Tim has told me a lot about you. How are you?"

I resisted the devilish temptation that flashed through my mind which was to answer that I was "pregnant by your fiancé, thank you very much. How are *you*?" and instead chose to be magnanimous (or cowardly, depending on which way you look at the situation).

"I hear congratulations are in order," I said, smiling and looking from one to the other.

"Blimey, news travels fast!" Tim said, obviously abashed. "We only announced it on Friday."

"You should know by now that you can't keep a good bit of gossip quiet for five minutes around here," I replied as sunnily as I could muster, adding, "Jane Bennett told me. She was at your party." Though I didn't mean it to come out sounding churlish – like where was my invite to your blasted party then? – that's exactly how it came out.

Tim looked taken aback for a moment, and I could see the cogs in his brain roaring into over-drive.

"I . . . er . . . I intended on calling you and telling you myself," he spluttered, "but what with one thing and another, I never got round to it."

"It's OK. Really," I said, genuinely wanting to make amends. "There was no reason for you to think you should have told me separately. It's been months since we broke up."

"I know," he carried on. "But I would have preferred you to hear it from me rather than school gossip."

"So, have you two set a date?" I knew I was making all the right noises, though the words were choking me inside.

"We thought next spring would be nice, didn't we, babe?" Amy answered, clutching at Tim's arm.

Tim looked a little bit dismayed by the way the conversation was developing.

"Anyway, I haven't seen you for ages," he said, changing the subject. "How are you?"

If we had been on our own and I thought there might be a chance that Amy was just a passing fancy rather than the person he was about to buy a sparkly rock for, then I might – just might – have been able to bring myself to tell him how I really was. As it was, I now realized that I shouldn't, couldn't and wouldn't *ever* reveal my true condition.

"Oh, I'm fine," I lied, "really well. I'm just looking for a birthday present for Shona."

"Of course, it's her twenty-first soon, isn't it?" Tim replied. "Oh well, wish her a happy birthday from me, won't you?"

"Sure," I replied quickly. "Anyway, I'll let you carry on choosing. I . . . uh . . . don't think there was anything I wanted for Shona in here anyway." I was backing out of the shop now, keen to get away. "I'll see you around," I added, and put my hand up in a little wave goodbye to them.

"Bye, Lucy. Take care." Tim smiled, while Amy gave me a little wave of acknowledgement.

As I reversed out of the shop I could see them framed in the large window of the door, a lovely picture of the perfect couple holding hands and smiling at me as I retreated rapidly into the street and walked away.

My last hope had disintegrated before my eyes and I felt desperately alone, with no one to confide in. Telling Tim had been a longshot from the outset, but now I knew the idea was a non-starter. I was going to have to cope with this thing on my own.

Chapter 8

"So, what are you wearing tonight?" Shona bounced up and down on my bed, eyes shining, unable to contain her excitement. You could hardly blame her. It was her twenty-first birthday and Dad had kindly allowed his eldest daughter to hold a party at our house to celebrate. Even more graciously, he'd agreed to vacate the premises for the night. Consequently, she had been bounding around the place like a young puppy for the entire day, enthusiastic and excited, and unable to settle down to any one task for more than a few minutes.

The upshot of this was a half-made plate of cheese and tomato sandwiches, loose, wafting balloons, not yet tied together let alone homed in ceiling corners, and cans of lager littered over the kitchen floor rather than on a table some-where. Obviously bored by such chores, Shona had decided it was time to accost her sister, who had been hiding away in her bedroom for most of the day. She had already paraded her choice of party wear for the evening and now wanted to know what I was planning to wear.

I hadn't given the idea any thought what-soever. Since I'd found out about being pregnant, I hadn't given anything much thought, to be honest. I felt totally numb, as though I was in some kind of pregnancy denial. I was aware of what was happening to my body, but chose to ignore it. It was the only way I felt I would be able to cope without having a complete mental breakdown. I knew I had no choice now but to get through the next few months as best I could. My plans after that were anybody's guess. I played out my life one day at a time, not daring to think about what lay ahead, living only for the moment, behaving as normally as was possible, but feeling a bit like an empty shell rather than a person.

"Oh, I dunno," I answered her question wearily. "I haven't thought about it. I'd much rather stay in my room for the night and let you lot get on with it. Have you made the sausage rolls yet?"

"No, you misery guts, I haven't. And it hasn't gone unnoticed that you haven't been hugely enthusiastic about this bash, nor that you've hardly left your pit today. But you can't hide in here; we'll need this room for coats, or private snogging or something."

"I know," I answered, "and I'm sure I'll enjoy it once I get going. It's just that it's so long since I went to a party – even if it is at our house – I think I've forgotten how to have a good time."

"Well, you've only got yourself to blame for that," Shona said frankly. "I always said it was a bad idea to let go of your friends when you started going out with Tim. You can generally bet the friends will last a lot longer than most boyfriends.

"Right, I can't sit around here ranting at you any longer," she continued. "I need to clear the living-room. You can come and give me a hand if you can be bothered."

I sighed. "OK, I'll be down soon. I just need to sort out what I'm going to wear."

She leapt off the bed and out of the room, leaving me standing in front of the open door to my wardrobe, scanning rails of clothes I could no longer dream of wearing. Half the reason why I didn't go out in the evenings was because I didn't have anything I could fit into. Having said that, so far, disguising the ever-growing bump was easier that I thought. I've never been into wearing clingy clothes during the day, preferring to feel comfortable in leggings or jeans and baggy tops, so hiding it wasn't such a big problem.

Having a large frame was certainly to my advantage. If I'd been five foot two inches and really petite I would have had no chance, it would have started showing almost straight-away. In fact I probably would have realized what was going on many weeks earlier. As it was, for the first time in my life I was grateful that my child-bearing hips were able to disguise my exploding waistline.

I finally decided on an oversized shirt and my largest pair of "loose fit" jeans, which now were more snug than roomy. Aware that I was going to look like I was off for a walk in the park rather than at my sister's twenty-first, I teamed the look with strappy high heels and loads of OTT jewellery. Then I slung the lot on a hanger on the wardrobe door and went downstairs to help Shona.

I found her not in the living-room as she'd said, but in the kitchen, tipping a bag of frozen party sausage rolls on to a baking tray.

"Ooh, at last," she said by way of welcome.

"You can finish the sarnies if you like, and I need to make an alcoholic fruit punch too, but I haven't got any fruit or juice, and we need to get all the furniture out of the living-room bar a couple of chairs."

"OK, OK," I said. "And what time is this do starting – midnight? Because we won't be ready before then."

"We'll have to be; I've told everyone to be here at seven-thirty."

"How many have you invited?"

"I dunno, I lost count. Fifty or sixty."

"What?" I gasped, goggle-eyed. "Does Dad know there's going to be that many people crammed into his little house?"

"Hardly," she scoffed. "I told him there'd be twenty at the most."

"Well, I hope for your sake he doesn't decide to come and see what's going on."

"Don't worry, I'll blame the extras on you."

"Then he'll *know* you're lying. Even Dad knows I haven't got that many friends."

"Have you invited anyone, by the way?"

"Don't be silly," I laughed. "Who am I going to invite?"

"Oh, for God's sake, Lucy, get a life!" Shona mocked, laughing. "You've got to be the most anti-social person I've ever met. I don't know what's happened to you, you've become so boring."

I felt riled by her accusations, however light-hearted they were meant to be. I decided to change the subject, not wanting to start a slanging match on her birthday.

"So do you want me to go out and get some stuff for the punch?" I asked.

"Please. I'll write you a list." Using her left hand to search a drawer for a pen and paper, while at the same time shoving sausage rolls in the oven with the right hand, Shona somehow managed the two jobs at once and then began making a shopping list while I buttered bread and lumped cheese slices in the middle to make reasonably edible-looking sandwiches.

That done, I was pleased to get out from under the feet of my stressed-out and hyperactive sister for half an hour. As always she was right. I did need to be more sociable. However, you could hardly blame me for putting everything on hold for a few more months, at least until this episode of my life was finally over. Only then did I think I would be able to become a normal teenager again.

By some miracle, we actually managed to have the house and ourselves ready with a few milliseconds to spare, so that I was just slapping on some lipstick when I heard the front doorbell ring for the first of many times. People were starting to arrive.

I jumped up from where I'd been sitting over one of those magnified hand mirrors that show up all your imperfections and stood in front of the full length mirror on the wardrobe. I peered at my face for the last time. I was wearing hardly any make-up, just a bold lipstick and a bit of clear mascara. In the last few days my skin had cleared up and was looking healthy again. My hair looked pretty good too, even if I did say so myself. It was as though my whole body had undergone an amazing transformation, from knackered old banger to shiny new model. It was a massive improvement, no doubt something to do with the change in hormones – a condition I wished I could bottle and sell and make a million pounds out of.

However, it was a pretty grim sight from the neck down. I know I was probably being too hard on myself, but it didn't matter which way I studied myself, I looked like I was about to take the dog for a run rather than helping host the party of the moment. *I'll be glad when it's all over*, I thought as I dragged myself down the stairs.

So many people seemed to arrive all at once that I spent most of the next hour or so opening the door to people and ferrying coats and things upstairs to Dad's room. I hardly had time to look in the living-room or kitchen to see how it was all going. It sounded good though; the noise blaring from the speaker system was resounding around the house, making the windows rattle and the walls thump to the beat of techno music mixed with garage mixed with soul and funk and crikey knows what else. I was quite enjoying my job as coat bearer; it meant I got to meet everyone as they arrived, have a few cursory words with them, take any belongings they didn't want to carry around with them, point them in the direction of the kitchen where the food and booze were, then leg it upstairs with aforementioned items, where I would loiter until I heard the doorbell go again.

This went on for an hour or so, by which time the place was beginning to heave and I was having a panic that we weren't going to be able to fit everyone in. Then the doorbell rang again and as I headed downstairs from the sanctuary of my bedroom I just prayed that there weren't going to be twelve or fifteen people outside, because there was no way they'd all get in.

However when I opened the door there was just the one person there.

I felt my jaw go slack at the sight of the divinely drop-dead gorgeous David (of the pop-star looks) in the doorway. I don't know why I was surprised to see him standing there – he was a friend of Ryan's, after all. To be honest, I hadn't given him any thought since the night Ryan and Shona had gone to the Comedy Club with him. I mean, so much had gone on in my life since then; he truly hadn't entered my mind. I guess if he'd called with the tickets we'd spoke about then things might have been a bit different.

Seeing him now made me tingle from my head to my toes. God, was he cute!

"Aren't you going to invite me in, then?" he smiled as I stood there staring at him like he was from outer space.

Taking my lack of response to mean I didn't recognize him, his face took on a look of total embarrassment as he added, "I'm David. We *have* met. You probably don't remember—"

"No, no, I do remember," I finally managed to splutter, "I just – oh I don't know, I was miles away, that's all. Come in."

I stood aside to let him pass and got a heavenly waft of expensive-smelling aftershave. Ooh, he was *so* good looking it almost hurt to look at him! I marvelled at how huge he was – at least six foot two inches and with shoulders like upturned rowing boats. I felt positively waif-like next to him (difficult, I know, in the circumstances).

He gave me a quizzical look as we stood in the hallway together, me not daring to breathe let alone speak.

"You look different from the last time I saw you," he announced, his brows knitted in consternation.

I blushed, dreading that he meant different as in larger round the girth, hoping that he meant different as in improved since I looked like I hadn't washed for a week on that occasion.

"Do I?" I said innocently, acting surprised.

"Yeah, you look sort of glowing, more cheerful than you did then."

I grinned. "Well, I'd just split up with someone the last time I saw you. I was feeling a bit sorry for myself and being a miserable cow, so that's probably why."

He laughed. "That's honest," he chuckled. "You're obviously over it then?"

"God, yeah," I chuckled. "He's getting married to someone else so I had to get over it."

David roared with laughter at this, which put me completely at ease. Maybe the evening wouldn't be so dull after all.

"Shall we get a drink?" he asked, motioning with the Tesco's carrier bag he was holding towards the kitchen.

"We-ell, I'm supposed to be doorbell and coat wallah for the evening."

"That sounds like a really exciting way to spend the night," he joshed with an exaggerated yawn. "What did you do to your sister to land that job?"

"Actually, I offered," I said meekly. "At the time it seemed like a good way to keep myself occupied in a houseful of people I hardly know."

"So you're not much of a party animal then?"

"Not really."

"Me neither. I like talking to people too much. I know it sounds really old and farty, but I can't stand it when you can't hear what people are saying above the music."

Now it was my turn to roar with laughter. "You're right, you do sound old and farty. You'll be telling me Celine Dion is your favourite artist next!"

"Actually, she is." It took a few seconds before I realized he was joking, then we both cracked up again.

Against all earlier expectations, I had a brilliant time at Shona's party. Although David knew loads of people there, instead of going off and talking to them or dancing or whatever, he stuck by my side for the whole evening. I was both flattered and dumbfounded by his attention. If I didn't know any better I'd think he was interested in me – you know, in a snogging way, not just a friendly way.

It hadn't gone unnoticed by Shona either. At one point when I had to go to the loo she followed me upstairs for a conflab.

"What's going on between you and David?" she demanded, her eyes on stalks.

"Er . . . nothing, really," I replied as casually as possible. "We're just having a chat."

"Are you sure that's all it is?" she giggled. "From the way he's looking at you I'd say he's got the serious hots for you."

Oh wow! So it *wasn't* just my imagination, Shona had noticed it too. It was all I could do to stop myself from kissing my sister, such was my happiness. But I deliberately played down my response.

"Nah, you're imagining it," I said. "We just get on. I like him."

"Pah!" she scoffed. "My foot. You'll be all over each other by the end of the night." And then she was off back down the stairs again, leaving me with a little glow of happiness in the region of my heart.

The evening whizzed by far too quickly. I didn't notice the mass of people packed into the house, far too many to be comfortable. And yet I was as cosy and content as I had been for a long time. David was really good company, easy to talk to, and drop-dead gorgeous (have I mentioned that before, by any chance?). I wasn't aware of the noise from the sound system, nor of the fracas that broke out between a couple of the younger lads who were tanked up on cider and scrapping over who'd had the last of the Diamond Ice. I didn't notice when people began drifting away home after midnight, or when Shona and Ryan disappeared to her room, or when there was just a handful of us left, then only David and me. When he finally announced that he ought to go home I was surprised to see the whole house deserted and that it was four-thirty in the morning.

"Blimey!" I exclaimed. "I had no idea that was the time."

"Me neither," he replied. "I thought it was only about eleven o'clock. I've got to be up at seven."

"Oops!"

He began heading in the direction of the front door.

"I'll walk you to the gate," I said.

He laughed. "Thanks. That's very chivalrous of you."

"Well, we don't want you getting lost on the way."

We strolled outside in silence, the chilly night air hitting us like an iceberg after the heat from inside the house.

"Thanks for a great party," David said once we were at the open gate. "I've had a really good time."

"No, thank *you* for saving me from being found buried under a pile of coats in my bedroom, having died of boredom."

We stood for a few moments, me not wanting the evening to end yet knowing that it must, and wondering what to say as a parting shot. I was in a strange situation, desperately wanting something to come of this evening, but petrified at the same time if it did. I mean, how long was I going to be able to hide the fact that I was going to have a baby? Not long enough, I was sure.

"You're good company, Lucy," he announced, making me blush. "I'm pleased I managed to keep you all to myself tonight. It's been brilliant."

"Aw shucks," I mocked. "I was thinking exactly the same about you."

"So can I call you some time?" he ventured. "We could go out for a pizza."

Oh, fab! I thought. *He's asking me out.* I'd

hardly dared dream he would, wondering if perhaps I'd been reading the evening totally differently to him. But no, he obviously liked me as much as I did him. It was the best thing to happen to me in ages.

I tried to keep my cool when I answered.

"I'd love to," I said, then grinned a smile as wide as the Thames, my delight obvious, attempts at staying cool abandoned.

We were almost unbearably close now. His left arm was brushing against mine and the tingling sensation it sent through me was like a massive attack of pins and needles.

He hooked a finger around one of mine and soon our hands were clasped together. He turned towards me and I took his other hand and we stood facing each other like that for a moment, studying each other's faces, looking into each other's eyes.

And then he kissed me.

It was a gentle, lingering kiss, which left my body breathless and emptied my mind of everything except the most wonderful sensation of the kiss itself. It was heavenly.

"Wow!" he whispered when we finally pulled away from each other.

"Double wow," I replied.

"I . . . er . . . I'd better go now, or I'll never

want to leave," he smiled, adding, "I'll call you," as he climbed into his beat-up Maestro, turned on the engine, gave me a little wave through the window and roared off down the street.

Chapter 9

I saw David on and off over the following
months. Nothing heavy, you understand – the
last thing I needed was to jump into another full-
blown romance like the one I'd had with Tim.
And I got the impression that David wasn't into
the idea of a serious affair either.

It was like we were two individuals who
happened to get on and who liked each other a
lot, but who also led separate lives away from
each other. It was a completely different
relationship from what I'd been used to. We had
a good time together, there was no pressure. I
think it suited both of us.

I never referred to David as "my boyfriend",
and I don't think I ever heard him introduce me
to anyone as his girlfriend. That said, there was

no one else in my life (not in the snogging sense) and I was pretty sure the same applied to him. I don't think I would have worried if he was seeing anyone else. I was perfectly happy to see him on a casual basis, no strings attached. I was actually terrified about getting into a proper relationship; I felt the urge to have a good time, experience a little bit more of life, before I settled down again.

Although we were seeing each other on a fairly regular basis, sex wasn't an issue – we just didn't have any. As far as I was concerned any kind of nakedness was out of the question in my condition; whenever he tried it on, I told him adamantly that I wasn't ready to sleep with him yet. Which was true, and would have been even if I wasn't pregnant. I would then inform him that if he wanted to have sex with someone he would have to go elsewhere for it. To which he always replied that it didn't matter, that he would wait, there was no need to hurry. I had no reason to disbelieve him.

I was acutely aware of the bulge in my stomach, and could hardly bear for David to go anywhere near it. Holding hands was great, because then I had some control over what his paws were doing, but anything which got near to an embrace was swiftly and deftly deflected so that my body didn't get within touching distance of his.

I got the impression that he thought I was really shy, both of guys in general and of my body. Which, when it came to the latter, was true, but not for any reason he would have considered. The thought of him coming into contact with the balloon-like appendage on my stomach and of perhaps working out what it was, actually made me shudder.

I was particularly worried because the creature inside me had developed the frightening habit of punching and kicking with such ferocity that the bump of a little fist or foot could be seen moving across my belly.

The first time I saw this happen was when I was in the bath one evening. I'd noticed, with great curiosity, the water rippling around my belly, then lay there amazed as my life turned into a scene from *Alien* where the creature bursts out of the hapless scientist's stomach. I remembered it being one of those scenes in the film where the entire audience jumps in shock-horror, and that was exactly what I did. It was terrifying. I was sure the baby was trying to get out, and even fleetingly wondered if there was any way it could escape. Through my belly button or something!

After that incident I went to the local library and started taking out books on pregnancy and birth, so that I could be more prepared for such bizarre events. Consequently, when I wasn't seeing David I spent a lot of time in my bedroom mugging up on my predicament. The more technical the books were the better as far as I was concerned. I needed to amass as much practical information on childbirth as was humanly possible in order to help prepare me for the inevitable day – or night – when I would go into labour.

I studied as though for an exam, which I suppose was what it felt like – the biggest, most important test of my life so far. By my hazy calculations, I was due to give birth sometime towards the end of June, right in the middle of my end-of-year exams at school. It meant I had a massive workload to get through, what with studying for three A levels too, and I kept having nightmarish thoughts of going into labour during an end-of-term exam and giving birth in full view of my entire school year.

I'd read that the average labour for a first-time mum was around twelve hours but could be as little as two or three, or as much as twenty-four, sometimes more. While the shorter option seemed the most agreeable, I was terrified it would happen during a three-hour English literature paper.

The other thing that worried me was whether I'd even realize I was in labour. I know it's supposed to be excruciatingly painful, and you'd therefore have to be pretty dim not to know what was happening to you, but even so, I'd heard stories of babies being born on the back seat of cars on their way to hospital, or of women's waters breaking while they were halfway round Tesco's and all this fluid gushing out over the shop floor. I'd be really humiliated if something like that happened to me.

The more I read, the more scared I became. Before I picked up my first medical book I was totally ignorant of childbirth. Giving birth appeared to be the most natural and normal thing in the world, which I guess it is, but I wasn't aware of how fraught with difficulties and mishaps it could be. I didn't realize that, compared to most mammals, women weren't actually built particularly well for childbirth. I decided that ignorance was indeed bliss, and wished I'd never bothered to pick up a book on the subject, instead letting nature take whatever it decided to throw at me on the day. Unfortunately, it was too late to unlearn the scary stuff I'd already assimilated so I had to plough on.

Something which gave me quite a bit of concern was the fact that I seemed to be smaller than the pictures of women I saw at the same stage of development as me. I wondered if my dates were completely out and that I was actually less pregnant than I'd assumed. I had barely put on fourteen pounds in weight when by rights the average pregnant woman would have put on about eighteen pounds or more at the stage I was supposed to be at.

It didn't stop me from looking like a weeble, although thankfully the only person blunt enough to comment on my expanding girth was Shona, who made bitchy and/or concerned comments depending on what sort of mood she was in. On one occasion she asked me when my audition for the Teletubbies was, on another she took me aside and announced that she was going on a health kick because she wanted to tone up her thighs (which, incidentally, made a couple of Twiglets look fat) and would I like to join her? I declined, saying I was perfectly happy with my size thank you very much, and could she get in extra chocolate bourbons next time she was doing the family shop, because one packet didn't last more than an evening, let alone a week? That shut her up.

I was also careful to make sure I was seen with

giant sausage rolls or family bars of Dairy Milk in my hand whenever I was in company, to keep up the troughing pretence. In reality I was eating very little, my fear of ballooning into an obviously pregnant hippopotamus overriding any desire to consume normal amounts of food.

I lived in fear every single day of being found out; when I went to bed each night, my secret still undiscovered, I would feel the relief wash over me. I was ticking off the days to the time when my life would resume some kind of normality.

After much soul searching, I had come to the conclusion that – assuming I could get through the birth on my own – when the baby was born I would take it to a safe place and leave it to be found by someone. I had the perfect place lined up – a local doctors' surgery a short walk from our house. I figured it would be ideal to take the baby there, considering the surgery was open from eight in the morning, and the people working there would know how to deal with anything if there was a problem with the baby.

I had no qualms about undertaking what might seem like such a foolhardy act; I'd sometimes read stories in the newspapers or seen reports on television about babies being found abandoned in doorways. There were plenty of mothers out there who either couldn't cope, or who had realized they'd made a mistake. For them, like me, this was the only way out. At least I would know that the baby was going to be cared for and loved by someone far worthier than me. And this way, no one need ever know I had been pregnant and I would be able to get on with my life as best as I could, as though nothing had ever happened.

I never once considered that I might feel some affection for the child I was going to give birth to. I didn't think of it as a living thing, a product of myself. Nor did I consider the natural instinct a mother has for her child, or the instant bond between them that connects them for a lifetime. I was ambivalent about the baby growing inside me – to me it was nothing more than an inconvenience, and I had no reason to believe my feelings would change.

I couldn't have been more wrong.

"I thought I might go to the fair this evening. Do you fancy coming along?"

It was a lovely warm afternoon in June and I was on the phone to David, discussing what we were each doing at the weekend (me revising, him partying) when he came up with the suggestion. The trouble was, I had no idea what he was talking about.

"Fair?" I said. "What fair?"

"At Dundry playing fields. It's been there all week. Haven't you seen it?" He sounded incredulous at my lack of observation, no surprise since Dundry was less than half a mile from my house.

"Er . . . no, I haven't been out much this week," I said feebly. "I've been staying in, studying."

"Well, it's about time you had a night off then," he replied cheerily. "What do you say?"

"Brilliant," I replied without hesitation. "Great idea."

"Six o'clock OK? I'll pick you up."

"I'll be ready."

"See you later then," he said and put the phone down.

How exciting! I thought. I know fairs are supposed to be for little kids but I've always loved them. I like the myriad sounds which hit you from every direction, and the sickly sweet smells of candy floss and toffee apples. Fairs are always a barrage on the senses and I love going back to my childhood and acting like a seven-year-old again. David had no idea what he was letting himself in for.

He was right, I did need a night off, although while he thought I was revising for my end-of-term exams, I was in fact cramming my head full of facts about contractions and umbilical cords and suchlike.

I gathered up the three medical books which were strewn about the room and put them back in their hiding-place, in a battered old vanity case under the bed. At a (very) vague guess I had two or three weeks to go before I was due to give birth and was beginning to feel a bit nervous about what might happen. It would do me good to get out and have a good time, to take my mind off things.

I decided to make a real effort, both for myself and for David. I fancied pampering myself something rotten and taking time and care over my appearance for a change. It sounds silly, going to a load of effort just for a trip to the fair, but I often felt under too much pressure studying to spend time spoiling myself for a date, and would often throw on the first thing that came my way when I opened the wardrobe.

I spent the next two hours getting ready – I hadn't made so much effort since I first started going out with Tim. I rifled through my clothes and spent far too long choosing something flattering yet casual and not too tent-like. I settled on my one pair of black pregnancy jeans that were perfectly normal in the leg but which had a lycra section rising from the hips to the waist to accommodate the bump. I wore them, an over-sized white shirt and a black leather belted, knee-length jacket that didn't meet at the waist any more but strangely looked like it was meant to be like that. I put a wash-in wash-out rinse in my hair, painted my nails for the first time in months, carefully applied a dash of make-up and was ready with minutes to spare.

When David turned up, he was visibly surprised by the girl who opened the front door to him.

"Wow, you look fab!" he exclaimed, looking me up and down approvingly.

He bent down and gave me a tender kiss on the lips and I went a bit wobbly and had to grab hold of his elbows to stop myself from tipping up.

We sauntered down the road hand in hand and made our way to the playing fields a few streets away. It was a lovely balmy evening, and I felt relaxed and content in David's company. He was easy to be around, good fun, and we were on the same wavelength.

You could hear the din well before we were even in sight of the fairground. Chart music blared out, waging a war with the more traditional piped organ sounds of the gallopers and the side-shows. Intermittent screaming of varying degrees could be heard almost incessantly above the babble of chattering adults and excitable kids. And the chug-a-chugging of the generators keeping the whole show going outdid everything in the noise stakes. Probably one of the most skittish of all the kids was me; I was so keen to get there, I let go of David's hand and went trundling down the hill towards the action, well ahead of him. He looked on, amused and a little puzzled by the sudden character change of his date.

"Come on, hurry up!" I shouted back to him as he sauntered behind me. "Or it'll be finished before we get there, and I want to go on *everything*." I waited for him to catch me up then I grabbed him by the hand again and practically dragged him along the pavement towards the entrance.

It was still daylight so the gaudy colours and flashing lights managed to look cheap and tacky rather than thrilling and enticing as they would later on, once the sun had gone down and the trashy effects came into their own.

"Ooh, what shall we go on first?" I asked David, wide-eyed at the sight of so many thrills to be had. "What's your favourite?"

"I like the Ghost Train the best," he grinned, "because it's so *not* scary, it cracks me up."

"Me too!" I agreed, genuinely amazed that he felt the same way as I did. "Come on then, let's go and find it."

We were still holding hands and I tugged David in the direction of the Ghost Train which I could just about see tucked away in a corner of the field, as befitting its (un)popularity. I thought it was really cute (in a girlie sort of way) that we both liked the same ride, and for the same reasons.

There was a small queue of seven- and eight-year-olds waiting patiently for the next train to appear, and when it emerged into bright sunlight from the darkened depths of ghosty land, it was empty.

We clambered into the back seat of the rickety train and waited for the next ride to begin. I was a bit warm so I took my jacket off and laid it across my legs, then grabbed hold of David's hand again. He helped set the spooky scene by telling me ghost stories and soon we were heading off on our murky journey into darkness at a slow, unsteady pace.

The entire ride was unintentionally hilarious. We had to stifle hysterical laughter as badly made skeletons and ghoulish shapes were hurled in our direction, only to whizz away at the last minute just centimetres from our bodies. Papiermâché gargoyles with the paint peeling off their faces loomed up at us, and cackling witches' voices came from nowhere to scare us on our way. We screamed in all the right places and cracked up completely when one of the kids announced in a loud voice, "This ride's rubbish! I want my money back."

I clasped David's hand in mock horror throughout and squeaked and squealed my way round the assault course of fiends and monsters. I hadn't had so much fun in months.

When the train burst through its final set of doors, we groaned in unison, disappointed that the fun was coming to an end.

"That was fab," I gushed. "Can we go round again?"

"No, we can't," he laughed. "That's enough excitement for one evening. You're all flushed."

David stood up and struggled out of the fragile wooden structure then held out his hand to assist my ungainly and rather wobbly dismount. As I stood up I felt that my jeans were damp. Funny, I thought. I hadn't noticed the seat was wet. I looked behind me to the black wooden seat and noticed that indeed, there was a damp patch where I'd been sitting. But not on David's side of the seat. *Strange*, I thought. *It looks like I've wet myself.*

Then it dawned on me. My waters had broken. I was going into labour.

Chapter 10

Oh my God! I thought. *This can't be happening to me.* I stood at the top of the steps leading down from the ride, too petrified to move.

Panic began to run through my body, rising up into my throat, overwhelming me. I was absolutely terrified. I ran my hand down the back of my jeans, wondering if perhaps I might have made a mistake, but no – my clothes were definitely a little damp. Worse was to come. As I stood rooted to the spot I felt a pop inside me and rush of liquid from within. Instantly, a kind of warm wetness seeped through my jeans, much more so than before. I felt no pain, nothing seemed amiss, but I knew exactly what was happening to me. The dribble had been the fore-runner to my waters breaking, while the rush of liquid I was now experiencing was the real thing.

David had leapt to the bottom of the stairs and was turning round now, no doubt wondering why I hadn't followed him. "Are you OK, Luce?" he asked, frowning. "You've gone as white as a sheet."

I gathered my thoughts together, the fear of discovery overriding all other concerns.

"I've suddenly come over all dizzy," I lied.

David walked back up the steps to where I was standing and took hold of my hand.

"You're absolutely freezing," he remarked. "Sit down."

I freed my hand from his and quickly put on my jacket, thankful for its length and the fact that it now covered up the top part of my legs and bum. A little dazed, I sat down on the top step, resisting the urge I had to run away and hide in my bedroom until it was all over.

"I think all the excitement of the ride must have got to me," I smiled wryly at David. "I really don't feel too well."

"Shall I get you a drink or something to eat?" he asked, adding, "Do you feel faint?"

"I'm not sure what it is," I lied again. "I think maybe I ought to go home."

"Sure," he replied. "I'll walk back with you.

What a shame though. We were having such a good time."

"Maybe we could come back another day," I said vaguely, trying to keep the conversation going but not really listening to what was being said.

"Yeah, good idea," David replied. "It'll be here over the weekend, I'm sure. See how you feel in a few days. Maybe you've got one of those twenty-four hour flu bugs that's been going around."

I wish that was all it was, I thought ruefully.

I stood up and took hold of David's hand. I was terrified he'd look down to where I'd been sitting; it must look as though I'd wet myself. I was so scared, I didn't realize the ferocity with which I was holding on to him.

"That's one vice-like grip you've got," he joked.

"Ooh, sorry," I said, releasing the tension in my hand. "I just feel a bit unsteady on my feet."

We walked home in virtual silence. I was concentrating on what was going on inside me, trying to tune in to any unusual movements or feelings. But there was nothing; the baby didn't seem to be in any huge hurry to get out.

I was so relieved when we got to my house, all I wanted to do was escape to the sanctuary of my bedroom.

"Sorry to ruin our date," I said weakly to David.

"No worries," he replied. "I hope you're feeling better soon."

"So do I. I think I'll go straight to bed."

"Is your dad around to make sure you're all right?"

"No, he's been on a sales conference for the last two days. He doesn't get back till tomorrow. Shona will be home soon though."

"Well, if you're sure you'll be OK on your own for a while. . . You make sure she looks after you when she gets in, won't you?"

"I will."

I gave him a kiss on the cheek and a weedy smile and made my escape into the house, grateful to be on my own again.

No sooner had I closed the door behind me than it happened. I felt a wave of pain across my stomach, like I had a belt on and someone was pulling it tighter and tighter until it couldn't be pulled any further. Then the belt was loosened again and my stomach went back to normal. The whole process lasted for less than a minute. It didn't take much working out that this was obviously a contraction, but bearing in mind that this was only the beginning, I was surprised at how uncomfortable it was.

I went upstairs to my room and changed out of my damp clothes and into a towelling dressing-gown. Then I began to run a bath, having the urge to lie in warm water which I'd read that so many women in labour felt the need to do. While I waited for the bath to fill I took one of my pregnancy books from under the bed and began reading the chapter called "The Onset of Labour".

Then I felt another contraction across my abdomen and had to stop reading to concentrate on what was happening. I looked at my bedside clock: seven fourteen p.m. – it had been fifteen minutes since the first contraction. The possibility of another twelve hours of this filled me with dread.

I took my book to the bathroom and lay in the bath avidly reading pages and pages of information I'd already studied a thousand times before, but which now took on a whole new – very real and scary – meaning.

I lay in the bath for over an hour, constantly topping it up with piping hot water from the tap. During that time I must have had five or six more contractions, each one a bit stronger than the last, increasing in pain as they came and went. I was conscious of the need to relax, which was difficult seeing as I was half scared to death by what was happening to me.

I put my book down and tried to think of something else, to take my mind off the long hours ahead of me. For the first time in months I thought about Tim and wondered what he was doing this evening, when his ex-girlfriend was giving birth to his child. I began to question my decision not to tell him about the baby. If he ever found out, would I be accused of denying him his right to know that he had a son or daughter somewhere in the world? Would he be angry? Hurt? Ambivalent? The truth was, I didn't know how he would react, which was probably why it was all for the best if he never discovered the truth.

Then I began to think about the baby I was about to give birth to. I became curious as to what sex it might be. I had an instinctive feeling that it was going to be a girl, which was odd because I hadn't even considered what it might be until now. And what about a name? Should I give it a name? I pondered. Yes, I decided instantly – I ought to. Everyone deserves a name. If it was a boy there was only the one choice: Noah, after Noah Wyle who plays Dr Carter in *ER*, my hero from my absolute favourite television programme. Girls' names were a little more difficult. After methodically going through a mental list which lasted at least two contractions, I finally decided on Ellie. I would have liked to have been called Ellie – it was so much more unusual than Lucy, of which there were three in my form class alone.

I felt the by-now-familiar pull of another contraction and gritted my teeth as it pulsated through my body. They were becoming really painful now, and according to my book, I wasn't even a third of the way there yet.

I clambered out of the bath and stumbled back to my bedroom. It was only eight-thirty p.m. It felt like I'd been in the bath for days. I sat on the edge of my bed and hunted through my CDs for some soothing music to take my mind off the task in hand.

Then I heard the phone ring. I couldn't decide whether to answer it or not, in case I had a contraction during the conversation and ended up chewing the receiver in agony. I did a quick calculation. So long as I wasn't on the phone for more than five or six minutes I should be OK.

I wobbled down the stairs and picked up the phone.

"Hello?"

"Luce, it's me." It was Shona. I'd wondered where she'd got to. She was usually home at about seven o'clock on a Friday evening.

"Hi! Where are you?" I asked.

"I'm in a pub. I met Ryan from work for a quick drink. But it's turning into a bit of a session, so I thought I ought to ring you to let you know."

"OK. Do you know what time you'll be home?"

"I might not. We're thinking of going to the Milk Bar later on and as it's nearer to Ryan's house than ours, I might stay the night at his place. You don't mind, do you?"

"No, of course not," I replied, hugely grateful that I was going to be left in the house on my own. "Have a good time."

"OK, I'll see you tomorrow. Got to go, there's about ten seconds left on the phone and I haven't got any more money. Have a good evening."

"You too," I said as I put the phone down. God almighty! I thought. If she knew what was going on in her house, she'd be having kittens.

The knowledge that I had the house to myself for the night came as a great comfort. It was sheer luck that it had happened this way, I'd often wondered how I was going to be able to give birth in a house with my father and sister under the same roof. This way, it couldn't have worked out any better.

I had quite a bit of preparation to do. Upstairs in my room once more I rummaged about in the back of the wardrobe and found the bag of necessities I had been gathering over the last few months. Thankfully, the medical books I had been studying were full to the brim of useful information on the stuff you needed for a home birth. While rummaging through the airing cupboard a while back I had found a couple of sheets which were never used. I stripped the bed and remade it with the old stuff. Then I took a piece of polythene sheet I had bought from a DIY store and laid that on top of the bed, spraying it with Dettox in the hope that it would kill off any germs that might be lurking there.

Next I brought out an old wicker basket of the sort you see old ladies carrying their shopping in. It had been lurking at the back of the shed in the garden for many years and I had decided it would do as a temporary cot for the baby to be transported in. I placed it on the floor by the side of the bed and took a blue cushion from the sofa which I put inside for the baby to lie on.

I had bought a baby's bottle and some SMA powdered baby milk, sterilizing tablets, a pair of scissors and a bulldog clip from a supermarket on the other side of the city. I boiled a kettle of water and put the scissors and clip in it with the tablets to sterilize them for when I would need them later on. I also boiled a small pan of water ready to use to make up the milk when I would need it for the baby to feed on after it was born.

Satisfied that there wasn't much else I could do for the time being, I went down to the living-room and switched the television on. I lay on the sofa and began channel-hopping, unable to settle down to watch any one programme. Every time I felt a contraction coming, I found myself curling up into a ball, with my knees up to my stomach and my head as near to my knees as I could get it. Only in that position did I feel like I was alleviating any of the pain, and even then it was more excruciating with each contraction.

In between times I would pace the house, wandering from room to room, looking for something to take my mind off what was happening to my insides – fiddling with the toaster, tidying the magazine rack, putting all my CDs back in their rightful boxes, then taking them out again and playing a few tracks before sorting them into alphabetical order and putting them away again. All the while I was doing my best to keep calm, to count the minutes between contractions, to breathe deeply and easily.

By midnight they were coming thick and fast. I was timing them at every three minutes, but the intensity of the pain and the length of each contraction made it feel as though they were continuous. As each one came to a peak I found myself burying my face in a cushion or the duvet or a pillow, depending on which room I had wandered into at the time. Then I would emit a gravelly howl of agony with my teeth and fists clenched.

I had never experienced such pain in my life. I found that I was spending a lot of time on all fours, or squatting in the most unattractive manner. Although it felt a fraction more comfortable like this, it didn't stop me from feeling like a wild, injured animal crying out in distress.

I gradually came to the conclusion that my baby wasn't going to be born in my bed, as I'd assumed it would. They always seem to be born like that on the television, but I now realized that the most comfortable position for me was squatting on the floor, however ungainly it looked. I went to my room and grabbed everything off the bed, transferring it all to the floor ready for the birth.

I can't begin to describe the excruciating agony I was going through by this time. I tried to compare it with any other pain I had experienced in my life. I remembered when I was about twelve years old I fell off a pony at riding school. It bucked like stink and I went flying through the air, and landed on my right arm. It broke the bone in two places, but as the breaks were so high up, almost to the ball and socket joint at the top of the arm, the doctors weren't able to put it in plaster, so I had to go around with no more support to my arm other than a sling for the next four weeks until the bones set by themselves. I remember it felt so bad that I spent most of my time wandering around the house whimpering with pain. Night-time was the worst, because no matter what position I tried to sleep in, it was impossible to get comfortable.

Compared with what I was going through now, that was like being slapped in the face with a piece of tissue paper.

At around two o'clock in the morning I had the overwhelming urge to push the baby out of my body. I had read that this was perfectly normal and meant that the baby was ready to be born. But I also knew that it was for the best if I could hang on as long as possible, resisting the feeling until I could bear it no more.

I've absolutely no idea how I managed to stand the pain, but as it became increasingly unbearable I finally pushed with all my strength. It was an enormous relief to be able to do something positive after all those hours of restraining from pushing against the great spasms ravaging my body.

Gradually I felt the baby's head appearing,

although as each contraction faded it would disappear inside me again, leaving me with the desperate feeling that it was never going to be born.

With each terrifying shove, it got a little nearer until, with one almighty push I felt the head pop out. The relief and release from pain was immediate. It felt like a champagne bottle popping its cork. I became aware of another contraction coming and shoved with all my strength once more. Out popped the shoulders and the rest of the body. My baby had been born.

It was a breathtaking experience. For a few moments I was too amazed to move, then, very gingerly I picked the baby up. I could see immediately that it was a girl. She wriggled in my hands as I held her close to my body and grabbed hold of the scissors and clip which were on hand nearby. I cut the umbilical cord, exactly where a picture in one of the books showed me, and used the bulldog clip to stem the flow of blood leaving it. I held her in my arms and looked at the clock on my bedside cabinet. Ellie was born on Saturday 9th June at three seventeen a.m.

Chapter 11

I was so overawed by what had just happened, I didn't quite know what to do next. She opened her mouth and gave a little wail, then closed her mouth again and just lay in my arms all bloody and mucky looking. She obviously needed to be cleaned up so I wobbled unsteadily to my feet and took her to the bathroom where I wiped her down with warm water and a sponge. Then I wrapped her in a hand towel and held her in my arms and went back to the bedroom, where I sat on the bed and stared at her.

She was so pretty. She didn't look like she'd just been born at all. I'd never actually seen a newborn baby before but I always got the impression that they all looked like ET. Everyone said they were always so wrinkly and ugly, like grumpy old men. But my baby was beautiful. Her skin was smooth and pink and she had a full head of black, straight hair framing her tiny face. She had long, dark eyelashes and a snub nose, and a little pink pouting mouth. And she was unbelievably tiny, much smaller than I'd expected.

She opened her eyes and looked at me for the first time. She had the most amazing sky-blue eyes and she looked at me coolly, as though she was assessing me, taking in my features, thinking, Ah! So you're the one I've been sharing my home with for these past nine months.

As I watched her my face broke into a smile. I couldn't help it, I was so amazed at this little thing I'd given birth to. I was glad I had chosen to call her Ellie – it suited her perfectly.

"Hello, Ellie!" I whispered to her. "Welcome to the world." I lifted my hand and stroked her cheek and she closed her eyes again and lay there as though she was the most contented person in the whole world. I couldn't take my eyes off her. I was completely in awe of her. It was difficult to believe that I had helped create this tiny, living, breathing, person, so perfect and pure.

She opened her eyes again, only this time they looked really angry. She knitted her brows together and her forehead wrinkled, then she opened her mouth and screamed her head off, a piercing, relentless shriek that turned her face purple with rage.

I was petrified. What had I done? What *hadn't* I done? Was she all right? Was she in pain? What on earth was happening? It happened so suddenly, with no warning, and I had no idea how to deal with it. I jiggled her up and down in my arms, going "Sssshush, sshuuush!" like I'd seen other mums do to their babies, but that just seemed to make her even more livid. Her little hands were now clamped into tiny fists which she seemed to be shaking at me furiously. I had no notion of what was going on.

Then it dawned on me: of course, she was probably starving. I grabbed the baby bottle from the dressing-table and put in a couple of measures of milk, then poured the water from the saucepan in on top. I put the teat and lid on, shook the vessel vigorously for a few moments, then took the lid back off and pushed the teat into the yawning chasm of noise that had become her mouth. She clamped her lips down on the bottle and began sucking furiously, peaceful once more.

Phew! Panic over. My speeding heartrate began to get back to its normal pace and I even had a little chuckle to myself at my obvious incompetence.

After just a few minutes, and no doubt tired from sucking, her little fists unfolded into hands again, her arms dropped from the prize fighter's stance they'd been holding and went limp, and her face once again took on angelic proportions. She was sleeping. I carried her gently to the basket and placed her inside, where she continued sleeping for the next couple of hours.

I was exhausted myself, but I didn't have time to rest; I had an awful lot of mess to clear up. I stripped the bed completely and put every scrap of bed linen, along with towels and tissues and flannels, into a couple of black refuse sacks, which I then put in the back of the wardrobe, ready for the next collection by the dustbin men.

I'd already decided that if Shona or Dad questioned me about the bags which were going to appear on the front doorstep in a few days' time, I would say I'd been having a major clear out of my bedroom and they were full of rubbish I wanted thrown out. I remade my bed with my usual bed linen, put the two medical books I'd been studying back under the bed ready to take back to the library, then gathered all the utensils I'd used for the birth and took them downstairs back to the kitchen, where I gave them all a thorough scrub before putting them back where they belonged.

Back in my room the only evidence left that a child had been born here was the baby itself, and she was still sleeping soundly in her basket.

Now I could concentrate on me. I was desperate for – and badly needed – a bath. As I ran the water I once again checked to make sure that Ellie was still asleep, which she was, then, just as I was about to ease my aching body into the water, I felt the most excruciating pain in the lower part of my abdomen. Bent double with pain, a wave of panic rushed through my body. *My God! I'm having another contraction!* I thought, and the prospect of another baby inside me fleetingly whizzed through my head. I was on the bathroom floor now, on my hands and knees, my fists and teeth clenched as I felt another contraction sear through my insides.

Of course! You stupid cow! I chided my overactive imagination as common sense took over. *It's not another baby, it's the afterbirth!* With everything that had gone on, and in particular the total amazement I had felt on giving birth, I had completely forgotten that my body had to expel the placenta bag my baby had been living in for the past nine months.

A third contraction and it was out, the

bathroom floor suddenly resembling a gory scene out of a horror movie. In the most matter-of-fact manner (I don't think anything will ever shock me again) I cleared the mess up and finally – thankfully – sank into the warm bath of water.

I lay there for a while, finally able to contemplate what had just happened. It was hard to believe that I had just given birth. I felt amazingly calm and peaceful about the whole thing, not how I'd imagined I would feel at all. Yes, it had been a traumatic experience, terrifying and painful, but for me the worst bit so far had been *after* she was born, when she'd started crying and I didn't know why. That was the first time I didn't feel like I was in control.

As I lay there washing the blood from my body I kept visualizing Ellie's face looking up at me and smiling. She really was beautiful. The bond I felt towards her even now was frighteningly strong. It was difficult to suppress these emotions, knowing in the back of my mind what I had to do next.

When I got out of the bath the water had been tinged red. I took a towel and began drying myself off, then looked at myself naked in the mirror, curious to see how different my body would look. I think I half expected to look like I hadn't ever had a baby, that once the bulge had been expelled, my skin would go back to its pre-pregnancy shape and texture.

How wrong I was! Sure, my stomach had lost its balloon-like shape only to be replaced with skin that looked and felt like a big pink blanc-mange hanging around my waist. When I poked it with my finger, the whole area wobbled merrily. It was gross.

I got dressed and made my way slowly back to my room. Walking was a painful exercise now, which I had to carry out slowly and methodically and without any sudden move-ments which might jar me in the pelvis.

I sat on the edge of my bed and looked through a chink in the bedroom curtains. It was still dark and time we were making a move. I began to rerun the next part of my plan through my head. I was going to make sure Ellie was well wrapped up, give her some more milk, then take her outside and put her on the GPs' surgery doorstep a couple of streets away. Then I would leave her and come home and become a normal person again.

"*I can't do this!*" The anguished voice spoke out loud, making me jump with surprise. But of course, it was me speaking involuntarily, though I had no idea I was going to say it until it came out. I began wrestling with my conscience.

What do you mean you can't do this? I chided. *You have to do this. It's the only answer.*

But it's my baby! I can't leave her like that.

You have to! I shot back, scared by my emotions. *It's for the best. It's the only way out.*

I've got to do this, I thought. *I mustn't back out now. I can't keep her. I can't suddenly produce a child from my bedroom and announce to the world that she's mine. I've come too far. If I had known I was going to have such strong feelings for her, then I might have done it differently. But not now, it's too late.*

And anyway, what kind of a life would she have with me? With no money, no prospects, nothing? She deserved much better than that. There were hundreds of couples out there who couldn't have their own children; they would love Ellie and care for her and give her everything she needed and wanted. They could offer her so much more than me. What could I offer?

Only love, the voice said.

I felt cornered, trapped. I was scared of my newly discovered feelings and of what I was planning to do. Until I'd actually given birth to Ellie, I'd never considered her as anything more than "It", a blob-like thing that was little more than an inconvenience to my life. I'd never thought about her as a person. Now, having seen her and held her and watched her open her eyes and look at me – her mother – I was no longer so confident that what I was about to do was the right thing.

I had to persuade myself to go through with it. There was no way out. It would be OK, she would be all right; I was doing the right thing, doing what was best for Ellie. *Do it now*, I told myself, *before you change your mind and it's too late.*

I slipped on a jacket and went over to the basket with my sleeping baby in it. I picked her tiny body up out of the basket and held her in my arms for the last time. She seemed so little now, so fragile and petite. I'd never seen such a small child before in my life. In fact, I don't think I'd ever been at such close quarters with any child under the age of two or three before. I'd never been into little babies – they always scared me. I was terrified I'd drop them. In the past whenever relatives had given birth, I'd always stayed well away until they were up and about on their feet. I was always afraid of the really tiny ones. And now here I was with my own little one and it felt like the most natural thing in the world to hold her, not frightening at all.

She stirred and her eyelids flickered open and

she lay there looking at me with those big blue innocent eyes.

I picked up the milk bottle and put it to her mouth, and watched as she fed greedily, slurping and sucking, completely content with her lot; then she drifted back off to sleep and I eased the bottle from her mouth, and laid her back down in the basket, putting the bottle in it next to her. I took another couple of hand towels and placed them in the basket on top of her, tucking them in round the edges so that the cold wouldn't find a way through to her. I prayed that she would be found soon after I left her, and that she was wrapped well enough for her not to get cold in the meantime.

I left the house, cradling the basket in front of me, praying that no one would see me as I made my way along my short, guilt-ridden journey. It was by no means a cold night, not for June, and I had Ellie so well wrapped I could just see her closed eyes peeping out from under the towels. I was sure she'd be snug in there, confident she'd be found safe.

I was beginning to feel a great discomfort in my abdomen and at the tops of my legs. I guessed that some kind of natural pain suppressants must have kicked in when I actually gave birth, ones which were now deserting my body, because I was sure I felt a lot more uncomfortable now than I had two hours ago when she'd first been born. It was as much as I could do to keep upright and walking in a straight line. I certainly couldn't hurry my journey – it was too painful for that.

The streets were empty, the air still as I walked. Although it was dark, the moon was three-quarters full and the street lamps well lit, so I was careful to keep my head down and my jacket collar turned up. That way, if someone did happen to look out of a window and catch sight of me, they wouldn't actually be able to recognize the figure walking along their road. It didn't stop me from being nervous of being spotted; the walk from my house to the doctors' surgery was in the middle of a residential area and I was acutely aware that I might walk into someone heading off for their early shift at work around the very next corner. Or that a car might drive past me at any moment and its occupants wonder what the limping girl with the food basket was doing wandering the streets at this time of the morning.

As much as possible, I kept stealing glances at Ellie as I walked. She looked so peaceful lying there asleep; she didn't have a clue as to what was happening to her. Good job too, I thought ruefully as I hurried on. I prayed that she wouldn't hate me for this when she was older, hoped that she might one day understand that I was doing this for the best – for my future, yes (that was undeniable) but for hers too.

Tears bit into the backs of my eyes as I walked along and I felt utterly wretched the nearer I got to my destination. Then, as I rounded a corner, I saw the surgery across the road in front of me. It was just a house really – a large Victorian semi-detached residence that had been converted into a general practice. It wasn't the same doctor that our family used – his practice was miles away, nearer to the house we used to live in – but I chose this one because I guessed that there would be someone there reasonably early to open up, as the first appointment was for eight a.m. (I'd already checked).

Also, I thought they would know what to do if there was anything wrong with my baby. This seemed unlikely now – she appeared to be perfectly healthy and content – but I didn't know that when thinking about where to leave her.

I liked the fact that there was quite a long path up to the front door of the house and that the pathway itself was well covered with trees and large shrubs, so I knew I wouldn't be too exposed to the world as I sneaked up to the door.

To me it seemed like a near perfect place to leave Ellie.

Now, though, as I neared the gate I was tearing my heart out. This was the hardest thing I was ever going to have to do. As I walked up the path I took one last look at Ellie. Holding the basket with one hand I took the other hand and kissed my finger. Then I laid it on her cheek as I put the basket on the doorstep.

"Bye-bye, baby Ellie," I whispered as I knelt before her. "Please forgive me."

Then I stood up, turned around and walked away.

Chapter 12

I made my way home, the feeling of emptiness and loss engulfing me with every step I took from the little girl I'd left behind. I thought I was doing the right thing, for Ellie's sake, but it didn't make me feel any the less guilty for my actions.

I found myself thinking about my own mother, who had abandoned Shona and me all those years ago. I began to wonder if she'd had a similar tussle with her conscience. I'd always considered her actions to be selfish, figuring that the only person who could possibly gain from them was her.

But maybe it wasn't as simple as that. I didn't know the whole story – I probably never would – but what if she believed we would be better off without her? What if she felt trapped in an unhappy marriage, and her only way out was to leave us and start all over again? What if, like me, it had been a heartbreaking decision made with the very best intentions? Maybe she wasn't so selfish after all. Whatever her reasons for leaving us like she did, it didn't make it any easier for me to come to terms with it. Would Ellie ever come to terms with the knowledge — assuming she was told one day — that her mother had abandoned her? Possibly not.

As I turned the corner to the street where I lived, I looked towards our house and stopped, a feeling of dismay seizing me by the throat. There was a car parked outside. What was it doing there? It hadn't been there when I left. I walked a little closer, trying to make it out in the gloom.

It was Ryan's car which meant that he and Shona were in the house. What were they doing at home? Shona had said they were staying at his house for the night, so why had they come back here?

My God! I thought. What if they'd come back an hour ago, less even? Imagine the scene they would have walked in on. . .

I could hardly bear to think about it. Even now I was frantically going through every room in the house in my head, making sure there was no evidence left as to what had happened. I was pretty sure I'd cleared everything away, so now all I had to hope was that Shona hadn't looked in on me, expecting to find me asleep but instead seeing an empty bed that had been freshly made up and didn't look like it had been slept in at all. I realized that the chances of her doing just that were slim – she never came to my room in the night – but I couldn't be absolutely sure.

The house lay in total darkness as I crept up to the front door and put the key in the lock as slowly and accurately and quietly as I could. I prayed that Shona and Ryan were in bed, oblivious to the person attempting to creep into the house at such a strange hour of the morning. I opened the door and slipped inside, closing it gently behind me and standing in the hallway at the foot of the stairs. The house stayed silent and I crept up the stairs in the dark towards my bedroom.

As I got nearer the top of the stairs one of the floorboards gave out what sounded like an ear-splitting creak as I stepped on it. I cringed visibly and wasn't at all surprised when I heard Shona cry out.

"Lucy? Dad – is that you?" Her voice was a little tense – maybe she thought I was an intruder.

"It's OK, it's me," I called out. "Just getting some juice from the fridge."

"You frightened me to death creeping around," she said grumpily.

"Sorry."

I got back to my room, went inside and gratefully closed the door behind me. I switched on the light, lay on the bed and surveyed a scene that was so very different from what had gone on here a few hours ago. There were posters on the wall, school books strewn about the place, a pile of soft furry toys on the floor in one corner, and clothes and shoes and make-up scattered around. It looked like your average seventeen-year-old's room.

It was like Ellie had never been there.

I must have fallen into a deep sleep because when I woke up fully clothed, sunlight was streaming thorough the chink in the curtains and my bedside clock told me it was past midday.

My first thoughts were of Ellie. I was sure she would have been discovered by now. Panic began bubbling up inside me. Where was she? Who was she with? Was she all right? I felt I had to know the answers to these questions, I needed to make sure she was OK. But why, when she was nothing to do with me any more?

I was the one who had given her up, I had

decided she would have a better life without me, so why was I so worried for her welfare now?

The answer was obvious: because I cared about her.

I had read about mothers bonding with their children the instant they give birth, but I never expected it to happen to me. Not when I didn't even want a child. But that's what had happened, and that was why I was now lying in my bed weeping almost hysterically into my hands, feeling so wretched and low and so full of hate for myself.

"Lucy! Lucy! Phone for you." Shona's voice rose up the stairs towards me, momentarily breaking me from my thoughts.

I cleared the choking feeling from my throat and shouted back.

"Who is it?"

"David."

"Tell him I'll call him back."

"He wants to know how you are. I didn't know you were ill. What's wrong?"

"Nothing's wrong. I'm fine. Tell him I'm OK. I'll call him later."

I heard muffled tones as Shona spoke to David. I yearned to be able to confide in one of them, to be able to let go of the dreadful jumble of emotions that were ripping my insides out. But I couldn't. I wasn't brave enough.

How did I manage to get myself into such a hole? I wondered. If only I'd had the guts to tell someone what was happening when I first found out all those months ago, I was sure I wouldn't be in this mess now. I would have had help and support and understanding. I should never have let it go this far without talking to Shona or Tim or Dad!

Now I felt I had no option other than to do the thing I'd flippantly thought would be so easy once I'd cast my baby aside. I had to get on with my life as though nothing had happened. Go back to school, study for my exams, have my big career, my wonderfully fulfilling life . . . it all seemed so meaningless now.

I changed into some old clothes and left my room to face the world once more.

Shona was in her pyjamas and a pink dressing-gown, sitting at the kitchen table eating cornflakes and watching an old black and white film on the telly.

"You're feeling better then?" she asked. "What was wrong?"

I slumped into the chair opposite her.

"Dunno really," I lied. "I was out with David and I started feeling dizzy and sick so I decided to come home."

"And were you sick?"

"No. Where's Ryan – still in bed?"

She shook her head. "He had to get up early to help his dad with something."

"Is Dad back from the conference yet?"

"Don't think so; I haven't heard him upstairs. He said he might not be back until early this afternoon. Apparently it's a four-hour drive from Solihull. Are you seeing David tonight?"

"Er . . . no, I wasn't planning on it. I might give him a ring later."

"I said you would. He sounded really worried when he rang. He's so sweet. Ryan says he's really into you. Can't think why."

I didn't respond, I didn't even hear what Shona was saying any more. I had stopped listening, my mind having drifted back to thinking about Ellie again. I had an overwhelming desire to go back to the doctors' surgery, just to make sure she'd been found, that she was safe and well and. . .

I felt tears welling up in my eyes again and I stood up rapidly to leave the room.

"What's wrong?" Shona demanded. "What's the matter?"

I didn't dare look at her, couldn't let her see me like this.

"Nothing," I said, wiping my eyes with my

hands. "I've got something in my eye. I'll just go to the bathroom to sort it out."

I fled from the room to the sanctuary of the bathroom upstairs, where I locked the door and sat on the loo seat and cried my eyes out for the second time in ten minutes.

I heard Shona stomping up the stairs and cursed her for being so concerned.

"Are you OK in there, Lucy?" she called. "You're acting really weird. Has something happened between you and David?"

"Please, can you just leave me alone?" I wailed through the door. "I'm fine. Honestly."

"OK."

I heard her footsteps disappear into the distance as she went back downstairs, and continued howling into a handful of blue toilet roll until my bum went numb from sitting on the cold loo seat, after which I retired to my room and carried on blubbing on the bed.

I must have dozed off, the exhaustion from giving birth consuming me once more. It was a fitful sleep, interspersed with a series of nightmares involving Ellie. Horrible scenes played in my subconscious – in one I saw her lying in my arms, screaming and screaming until someone took her away from me and I stood crying and calling out to her but she never came back; in another I went back to the surgery to get her and the basket was there but Ellie had gone; in a third she was toddling about in the garden of a posh house playing with a family, and I was trapped on the other side of a huge pair of iron gates, trying to get her attention to make her come over and see me. She knew I was there but she just looked at me and laughed and carried on playing.

When I woke up I was bathed in sweat, my duvet and pillows in a jumbled, messy heap from where I'd been so restless in my sleep. I had an overwhelming feeling of loss in the pit of my stomach and an unbearable ache in my heart. I wasn't sure how much more of this I could take. I really felt like I was cracking up.

I heard a gentle knock on my bedroom door.

"Tea's ready," Shona said. "Are you coming down?"

"I'm not really hungry."

"You should have told me that before I made it. Dad's back. At least come and say hello."

I dragged myself out of bed and glanced at myself in the mirror. I looked dreadful, a pasty face and eyes red from crying. I didn't care. Nothing mattered.

I skulked downstairs to the kitchen where Shona and Dad were sitting over eggs and chips, the telly blaring away to itself in the background. I managed a weak smile at Dad and asked if he'd had a good trip, then sat in front of the remaining plateful of food and tried to join in with the family tea.

But the mere sight of food made me feel sicker than sick. And the prospect of playing happy families made me feel even worse. I was living a sham existence. My whole life from now on was destined to be one big lie. I couldn't believe what a fool I'd been to believe that I could continue with my life like this, after giving away my baby like an old unwanted bicycle.

I looked up from my plate of food and glanced at my father and sister, munching away, oblivious to my plight. What would they think of me if they knew what I'd done? In a way, I was desperate to blurt out what had happened, to relieve myself of this huge burden that was destroying me from the inside. My gaze moved over to the television set which was placed on a shelf above our heads. The pictures on the screen blurred in front of my eyes as I stared through the set, focusing on some distant point far away. I overheard snatches of words as the local news headlines were announced, and became vaguely aware of what was being reported.

And then my world stopped turning as I snapped back to reality. There was a report on the news about the baby abandoned on the surgery steps of the general practice at Middleton Road. When I saw the pictures of my baby on the screen and heard a policewoman showing the basket and the cushion and towels found with the little girl and appealing to the mother of the child to come forward so that she could get help – well, it was all too much for my already unstable frame of mind.

Stunned, I dropped my cutlery, and as my knife and fork clattered to my plate, Dad and Shona's heads jerked in my direction. I didn't care that they were both looking at me in surprise. It didn't matter any more. Nothing did. Scraping back my chair I leapt up from the table and escaped noisily from the kitchen. I heard the clatter of chairs behind me and Shona's voice saying, "Don't, Dad – I'll go," as I headed for the front door. I didn't know where I was going to go once I left the house.

"Lucy! Lucy! What's wrong? What is it?" Shona's voice rang out. She sounded frightened, out of control, just as I was. I got to the closed gate at the end of the path and fiddled with the latch, trying to make a hasty exit, like a thief leaving the scene of the crime. It gave Shona enough time to catch up with me, to grab me by the arm and spin me around to face her.

"Look," she said. "I don't know exactly what's going on here, but surely it can't be so terrible that you can't speak to me or Dad about it. I've never seen you like this before, Luce. You've been acting really weirdly for weeks now. If I didn't know any better I'd say it was something to do with that report on the news. Is it? Is that your baby? Is that what all this is about. . ."

Her voice trailed off as she looked right into my eyes, waiting for an answer, expecting nothing but the truth.

I studied her concerned, panicky face and saw the image of myself in it. I felt the tenseness of my body crumple and fall apart. I felt utterly desolate and desperate. I put my hands to my face and began sobbing uncontrollably.

I nodded, and a muffled "yes," broke from my throat.

Shona wrapped her arms around me and hugged me, a big, strong, comforting embrace. I fell into her arms and she stroked my hair with one hand and rocked me gently in her arms.

"Ssshush, sshuuush!" she said. "Don't worry. It's all right. You'll be OK, I'll sort it out."

"H-h-how can you?" I sobbed. "I've done the m-m-most terrible thing. I'll be p-put in j-j-j-jail for this."

"No, you won't," she smiled. "Come on, let's go back inside. You can tell me everything that's happened."

"Wh-wh-what about Dad? He'll kill me."

"No, he won't," she said definitely. "He'll understand, I promise you."

The relief I felt at knowing that I no longer had to carry the burden of such a huge responsibility on my own was extraordinary. It didn't stop me from being terrified of the consequences of my actions, but it did make me feel as though it might be a little more bearable.

We walked back inside the house to where Dad was standing in the doorway, looking frantic with worry.

"What's up, love?" he said, concern written on his face, sympathy in his voice.

"Let's all go and sit down," Shona directed. "We've got a lot of talking to do."

We trooped into the living-room and Dad sat on one of the chairs while Shona propelled me to the sofa and sat me down, then sat next to me and held my hand in hers.

I told them everything that had happened over the last nine months. As I spoke even I could hardly believe what I'd been through, it sounded so unreal. I felt like I was discussing someone else, that I was just an observer. It was difficult to believe that all these things had happened to me.

Shona and Dad didn't pass comment at all while I talked, although the expressions on their faces went from amazement to dismay to shock to concern to compassion and back again.

When I'd finished explaining I looked down at my hands. I couldn't face looking at Dad, I didn't dare to think what he was going to say about all this. But I did realize that whatever his opinion was it couldn't make me feel any worse. I was already at rock bottom.

When he came over to where I was sitting and put his arms around me I burst into tears again.

"My poor little girl!" he murmured. "You've really been through it. You'll be all right now though. I'll take care of you."

Hearing him say that made me cry even more.

"Wh-what about Ellie?" I sniffed. "Who'll take care of her?"

"We-ell," he said, "I expect that depends on you more than anyone. I'm no expert but I would think that the best place for a baby is with its mother. So really it's down to you and whether you feel able to look after her."

"Oh yes, I do!" I implored them. "I want her back so much. I've thought about nothing else all day."

"You'll need to think long and hard before you

make a decision like that," Dad replied sensibly, "and I don't think now is the right time to be talking about it. All sorts of people will need to be informed about this, and I expect you'll be asked a lot of difficult questions in the next few days. But we'll take one step at a time. The first thing we need to do is let the police and the hospital know."

He took both my hands in his and looked at me intently. Then he spoke again, his voice soft and full of compassion.

"The one thing I don't understand is why you never told Shona or me."

"I think I thought that if I didn't talk about it then maybe it wouldn't be true," I replied. "But it *was* true. And I was so scared. And then I realized that I'd come so far that I didn't feel able to tell anyone. So I just carried on, pretending it wasn't happening to me. And anyway, I was so sure you'd be mad at me, both of you."

"Poor Luce!" Shona said. "You've had a terrible time of it really, haven't you? I still can't quite believe what's happened. I'm amazed. I didn't even realize you were pregnant. It only clicked when I saw the stuff found with Ellie and I recognized the cushion. I was wondering where it had got to earlier today when I was tidying up. That's when I worked out that it was you."

"So I wasn't as careful as I'd thought," I smiled ruefully. "I'm glad I've told you both; it's a huge weight off my mind. But I'm terrified they'll say I'm an unfit mother and won't let me have Ellie back.

"Don't you worry about that," Shona assured me. "Once they understand what you've gone through, I'm absolutely sure you'll get her back."

Chapter 13

Things began to happen really quickly after that. Dad got straight on the phone to the police and within the hour there was a patrol car sitting outside the house and a knock on the door. He got up to let the occupants of the car in. Before coming into the living-room, they stood talking in the hallway for ages; all I could hear was the muffled tones of my dad's voice interspersed with female voices chipping in now and again. Finally, a uniformed police woman and another woman were standing in the living-room being introduced to me.

"Lucy, this is WPC Karen Styles and Lesley Harman from Social Services," Dad explained.

"Where's Ellie?" I demanded. I don't know

why, but I expected them to have brought her with them.

"She's still at the hospital," Lesley Harman replied. "Don't worry, Lucy. She's safe and well. She's a beautiful baby."

"I know. Can I go and see her?"

"Of course," she said. "We just wanted to come and have a talk with you first, then you can come with me and see your little girl."

The woman had soft features and a soothing tone to her voice. She oozed sympathy and wasn't at all hostile which, in a way, I think I'd half expected.

"Please, sit down," Dad said, adding, "Shona, why don't you make some tea for everyone."

Shona got up and disappeared into the kitchen while everyone else eased themselves into comfy chairs. Dad came and sat next to me on the sofa and held my hand for support.

"So, where do we go from here?" he asked, squeezing my hand as he spoke.

Lesley Harman took charge of the situation. "Well, obviously the welfare of Lucy's baby is of paramount importance to us. And I need to begin to assess Lucy and her ability to look after her baby. In order to do that, what I'd like to do, if this is all right with you, Lucy, is ask you to tell me just what you told your father and sister earlier. Do you feel up to doing that?"

I nodded. I actually felt really tense, like I was on trial and that whatever I said would have a huge bearing on whether they let me have Ellie back. The notion that my responses now might decide whether I had a future with my baby or not terrified me and I felt tears well up in my eyes and began to whimper again.

"Don't worry, sweetheart," Dad said, putting his arm around my shoulder. "It'll be fine."

"If you don't feel up to it now we could arrange to come back later, if that's what you'd prefer, Lucy," Lesley said.

"No, it's OK," I sniffled. "I'd rather get it over and done with. The sooner I do that, the sooner I'll be able to see Ellie again."

Between little gasps as I tried to steady my voice I once again related my story, explaining everything that had happened to me, articulating my thoughts and feelings whenever I felt able. Like Dad and Shona, the two strangers sat and said nothing. For the most part I kept my eyes firmly on the carpet, but when I did glance up to look at one or the other of them I could see nothing but compassion written on their faces.

While I was talking Shona had come back into the room laden down with a tray of tea things. She came and sat on my other side and took hold of my other hand, then as I finished my story she whispered "Well done!" and gave me a big hug.

"It's an amazing story, Lucy. You've obviously been through a lot," Lesley acknowledged. "Now, if it's all right with you, Karen and I would like to ask you some questions. You don't need to answer them all now. You can take as long as you want to think about what you want to say."

I took a mouthful of tea and nodded. "OK," I said, "I'll answer anything I can."

The policewoman turned to me and spoke. "Have you thought about whether you're going to tell the father, Lucy?"

"I don't know."

"If you do, he also has a responsibility to provide for your child. You do realize that, don't you?"

"Yes," I replied, "but he hasn't got any money; he's just a student like me."

"That may be the case now, but in the future when he's working he will be in a better position to provide for you. It's something you ought to consider seriously. You'll need all the help you can get."

"Plus," added Lesley, "you need to look at it from Ellie's perspective. If you don't let her have access to her father, are you denying her the very different kind of input and emotions a father can bring to a relationship? Would it be fair to withhold that from her?"

"I know," I agreed. "Everything you say is absolutely right. Look, I realize I've made a real mess of my life, and I regret it more than any of you will ever know. But all I want now is to get my baby back. That's all that matters to me."

"Of course you do, Lucy," Lesley sympathized. "We just need to talk with you to be sure that you're aware of the full picture. It's not going to be easy for you from now on. You're in your first year of A levels, aren't you? Have you thought about whether you're going to finish your schooling?"

"Er . . . no, school hasn't been uppermost in my mind recently. . ." I said weakly. "But . . . er . . . I guess it would be stupid to let it all fall apart. I mean, I don't want to give up on my A levels altogether. Perhaps I could just put them on hold for a while until I get more settled with Ellie."

She smiled at me. "That's very sensible. I'm sure you can sort something out to continue on a part-time basis, at your own pace. It won't be easy though; you do realize that, don't you?"

I nodded and she smiled again, before turning to Dad to begin asking him what his feelings were.

"Would you be happy for your daughter and her baby to continue to live with you?" she asked.

"Absolutely. I don't have a problem with that at all. Obviously it would mean a lot of changes around here, but we would cope, wouldn't we Shona?"

"Definitely," Shona said emphatically. "It wouldn't worry me at all. If that's what Lucy wants, then I'm happy to stand by her decision."

"Of course a baby puts quite a financial burden on a household. . ."

"I've already brought up two girls," Dad blustered a little indignantly, "so I think I'm in a position to know how much they cost. Financially I'm probably in a better position now than I ever have been. That's not something you need to worry about. Ellie won't want for anything."

"What baby equipment do you have? A cot, clothes, sterilizer for baby bottles?"

"Absolutely nothing at the moment," Dad said, smiling wryly. "But that won't be a problem. I'll buy everything she needs immediately."

"Actually," Shona cut in, "a friend of mine at work has got a load of baby stuff she wants to get rid of. I can give her a ring."

Lesley smiled and nodded and said "Good", then turned back to me.

"Well, Lucy, do you have any questions you want to ask either of us?"

I shook my head. "Can I go and get Ellie now and bring her home?"

It was then that she hit me with the bombshell. For the first time since we'd met she put on a more authoritative voice.

"I'm not sure you quite understand what's going to happen, Lucy," she explained. "Obviously we'll have to monitor the situation fairly closely from now on. Although you've been through a lot, we can't get away from the fact that you abandoned your baby. Ellie's welfare is of the utmost importance to us. You'll need to agree to work closely with a social worker who'll monitor your and Ellie's progress over the next few weeks. You'll also need to agree to have counselling to help you get over this period of your life. In the meantime, Ellie will go to foster parents until we all decide that you are fit and well enough to look after her full time."

"Wh-what do you mean?" I stuttered. "You're fostering her? Why?"

"Because, as I think I've said before, your baby's welfare is the number one priority. And while I don't doubt your good intention to look after her, we have to be absolutely sure of her safety. She'll be put into temporary care with a lovely family we've already contacted. They don't live far from you. You'll be able to visit her every day, you'll be shown how to look after her, and then, when you're able to, you can bring her home."

"But I can look after her now! Other young mums manage—"

"But with all due respect, most young mums don't leave their babies on doorsteps, for whatever reason."

I coloured bright red and looked down at the floor. Of course, she was absolutely right. I was Ellie's mother, but I hadn't exactly acted in the most responsible manner since she'd been born, had I?

"Look, Lucy," Lesley continued in her soft voice, "it's not as bad as you think. So long as you realize that we want to help you and Ellie as much as possible, and we co-operate with each other all the way down the line, then I don't envisage too many problems. You could have Ellie home with you in a couple of weeks. Is that acceptable to you and your family?"

I looked from Dad to Shona and back again.

"Of course, we'll go along with whatever's best for Ellie," Dad said without hesitation. Shona nodded vigorously in agreement.

"And what about you, Lucy? You're the one

who'll have to co-operate the most. What do you think of that?"

"So long as I get Ellie back, I'll do anything. Believe me, I'm never going to let her go like that again."

"Right then," she said, standing up. "I'm sure you're keen to be reunited with your baby. I expect a doctor would like to check you over too to make sure you're healthy, if that's OK. Would you like to come to the hospital with me now?"

I think the look of delight on my face got the message across fairly obviously.

"I'd love to," I exclaimed.

We all walked out into the fading afternoon sunlight. Already a few people in adjacent houses had found something interesting to look at in their gardens, and I saw a few curtains fluttering as I made my way to the police car. I smiled to myself. Soon the news would be the talk of the neighbourhood. I didn't care – nothing mattered as long as I got Ellie back.

"Would you like Shona or me to come with you?" Dad asked as we got to the patrol car.

"Would you come with me, Dad?" I begged.

"Of course I will. I'm as keen as anyone to see my new granddaughter."

"Thank you," I said simply. "You don't know how much your and Shona's support means to me. I'll never be able to thank you enough for this."

Dad held out his arms and I fell gratefully into them. We didn't speak any more, we just stood hugging on the pavement for a few moments. I went over to Shona and embraced her too, then Dad and I climbed into the back of the police car ready for the short journey to the hospital.

Settled in the back of the car, he took my hand, patted it, and held it for the entire journey. I don't think I'd felt so close to him for a long time I began to see the parallels between what was happening to me now with my own mother's life. Not for the first time, I wondered why she had walked out on us. I felt compelled to ask.

I turned to face Dad and spoke.

"Why did Mum leave home?" I asked, adding, "I know you've said it was because she didn't just want to be a wife and mum any more, but was that it? There isn't anything you've never told us?"

"Not really," he shrugged. "But if I'm honest I guess the truth *is* a bit more complicated than that. Before you and Shona were born your mum was very good at her job, highly motivated, she worked hard and had the potential do very well. But she wanted children too – we both did. I guess she thought she could do it all – run a family *and* have a career – but eventually she had to admit she couldn't split her life between the two, so she gave up her job.

"What you've got to remember is that this was before you had your equality for women and New Men or whatever it is you call them these days. If we were your age today she would have undoubtedly earned more than me and I would probably have stayed at home to look after you girls. But it wasn't like that then. Over the years it began to eat into her and she started to resent her life. She wanted more. She saw me plodding along as an OK but not hugely successful sales-man and knew that, given the opportunity, she could do so much better than me.

"Then she met Michael Redman. . ."

His voice trailed off and he turned away from me and stared out of the window of the moving police car. Dad had never mentioned the name of the man Mum had gone off with before. It obviously hurt him even to think about it.

"It's OK, Dad. I'm sorry, I shouldn't have asked—"

"No, love, don't worry. You have a right to know."

He cleared his throat and carried on. "This Michael, he was a businessman, the flashy sort – had fingers in lots of pies. They started having an affair, then he offered your mum a job heading up a new company he was setting up in Spain. Understandably, she jumped at the chance, upped and left one weekend. Haven't seen her since."

"Has she ever contacted you?"

"A couple of times. And the last I heard the company was a huge success with a turnover in millions. She got what she wanted, I suppose."

"I still don't see why you're not angry with her, why you don't hate her."

"I was angry. For a long time. Not any more though. I understand why she did it, just as I think I understand why you did what you did."

He gave my hand a little squeeze again.

"And anyway," he went on, "she left me the two most important things in my life: you and Shona."

Choking back tears, I gave him the broadest of smiles and a kiss on the cheek. We said nothing more for the rest of the journey – we didn't need to.

As we got nearer to the hospital I started getting butterflies in my stomach and my hands wouldn't stop shaking. I was desperate to see my baby again but at the same time I was scared too. Scared that once I got there, she would take one look at me and start screaming her head off because she didn't want to be with me. Or that the overpowering feelings I'd had for her since she'd been born would mysteriously disappear and I would be too frightened to go near her.

I needn't have worried. Once we got to the maternity unit all fears were overtaken by my desire to see Ellie again. Dad and I were directed to a little office which housed just a desk and a chair and an examining table while Lesley went to inform interested parties what was going on and the policewoman wandered off somewhere. About ten minutes later Lesley came back with a lady doctor.

"Before we bring Ellie to you," Lesley said, "Dr Lyster would like to examine you, just to make sure that you're well. Is that all right?"

I nodded. For the first time that day, Dad looked a bit embarrassed; he cleared his throat and left hastily. I spent the next ten minutes on an examining table being prodded and poked and asked by the doctor how I'd coped with the birth and delivery of the baby. She seemed genuinely interested – and amazed – by my explanations of medical books and bulldog clips and pans of boiled water. She concluded that I had come to no harm from my do-it-yourself home birth, but suggested that in the future I make use of the National Health Service, for my sake as well as my baby's. I smiled wryly and promised I would, then she left the room and Lesley came back in with Ellie lying in her arms, Dad following behind, a huge smile on his face.

"I think this is what you've been waiting for, isn't it, Lucy? And Ellie too, I'll bet."

She came over to where I was sitting on the edge of the examining table and put my baby in my arms. Tears slid down my face as I cuddled her. She was asleep, looking just as I'd remembered, totally content and without a care in the world. I felt a surge of emotion run through my heart as I watched her, the bond I had felt so strongly when I first held her in my arms instantly reconnected. I was completely in awe of her. A few seconds later Dad came over and peered at her, a look of utter joy painted on his face.

"What are you thinking, Lucy?" Lesley asked.

"I think she's wonderful," I said simply. Then the tears turned from relief to ones tainted with guilt as I thought about what I'd put her through so soon in her life.

"I can't believe I left her like that," I sobbed. "I'll never be able to forgive myself."

Lesley came over and put her arm around me. "Don't tear yourself apart over it," she said. "Try and put it behind you. What's important now is that you shower her with all the love you've got to give."

"Oh, I will!" I said, kissing her gently on the forehead. "You don't need to worry about that."

"Good," she said. "Well, you'll be pleased to know that I've just spoken to the foster family and they're happy for you to take Ellie home for an hour or two, so that you can get to know each other again. I'll stay with you, of course, then we'll walk the short journey to their house. It's only ten minutes from where you live, so you won't be far away from Ellie. Like I say, we'll play the next week or so by ear, to see how you're getting on, then, at some point, you'll be able to have her with you permanently. OK, Lucy?"

I nodded, stood up and made my way towards the door, still not daring to tear my eyes away from her in case she disappeared again.

"Come along, Ellie," I whispered. "Let's go home."

Epilogue

That all happened eighteen months ago.

Ten agonizingly long days after she was born, Ellie and I were permanently reunited. We haven't been apart for more than a few hours since.

And today? Today she is better than I could ever have imagined: wonderful, a walking, talking, cheerful little thing who never fails to brighten up my day. She's very much her own person, with a strong character and little quirks and personality traits, likes and dislikes, grumpy days and good days.

That said, if I could have my life again, would I do anything differently if I possibly could? Well, yes I would. Don't get me wrong: I don't regret having Ellie, but I do feel young to be a parent. My life had hardly begun when I became a mum, and while it's by no means over, it's certainly gone along a very different path from the one I'd expected.

I now realize that the very best thing about being a young person – which you probably don't realize at the time – is that you are Number One. Top dog. The world spins on its axis. Around you. When you have a child, your child automatically takes the top spot. Has to. You can no longer be self-indulgent; you have to put your baby's needs before your own; you have to be totally selfless.

Having a baby at seventeen is tough. Undoubtedly, I've lost a great big chunk of my life. My carefree teenage days are gone for ever, to be replaced by lorry-loads of dirty nappies, gallons of baby sick and years of sleep deprivavation. I'll never get those years back again.

I still study part-time, but the big career plan will have to come a little later in life than I expected. I'm under no illusions. I realize that when I do become one of the thousands of young jobseekers out there, I'll be at a huge disadvantage. Finding employment is hard enough, but imagine what it must be like when you're a single mum to boot.

If I could change anything it would be Ellie's relationship with her father. I gave a lot of thought to what the social worker said about Tim having the right to know, so that Ellie needn't be denied the opportunity to have some input from her father in her life, if that was what he wanted. As it happened, that wasn't what Tim wanted at all.

Understandably, he was staggered when I informed him about her, and it took a long time for him to come to terms with the idea of being a father at such a young age. I thought I'd handled telling him really well. I didn't put any pressure on him to come and see her, I just presented him with the facts, then said it was entirely up to him how he dealt with them.

In the back of my mind I hoped that he would want to be a part of Ellie's life, that he would want to have some say in the way she was brought up, to share the wonderful experiences I witnessed on a daily basis. I was at pains to stress that I didn't expect him to come back to me (in truth I didn't want him back, though I never said as much). But I was happy for him to spend some time with her, you know, on a part-time basis.

He wasn't interested. He wrote me a letter, saying how his life had moved on so much since we'd split up, that he didn't have any room in his life for Ellie. He "sympathized" with my situation and said he was grateful that I had told him of her existence, but that he wasn't ready to make an emotional commitment to fatherhood. He sent me a cheque and promised a monthly payment, to increase along with his income. To give him his due he's been as good as his word, but I was saddened by his decision.

I figured it was his loss.

Fortunately, Ellie has enough doting men in her life. There's Dad for one, who's developed a new lease of life since she's been around. No more late nights at work or the pub or overnight conferences for him. He's gone from being a dad who spent a lot of time away from home – I guess as much because he felt that at our age we didn't need him around any more – to being back in the evening well before Ellie's bedtime, usually with some silly toy or squeaky book for his first granddaughter. She's been great for the Hamilton household. It doesn't feel like we're fragmented any more – we're a lot closer, like a real family again.

And of course there's David. I never expected things to work out with him, especially after the way I felt I'd deceived him all the way down the line. But he coped with the news incredibly well, in a measured, accepting fashion, and has been a great big rock of support ever since. He's at university now, 120 miles away, but we still see each other at odd weekends and during term recesses, and he sends Ellie cards and presents. He thinks she's great, and she adores him. Do I see us going anywhere? Who knows? I try not to count on anything in life any more.

Ultimately, much good has come out of what once seemed like a desperate situation. I can't pretend life isn't tough – believe me it is. Sometimes I'm so exhausted I feel like the walking dead, and I'd be lying if I didn't say how much I envy the lives other kids my age lead. But when I look at my little girl with her purity and innocence and wholehearted love for me, I realize how fortunate I am to have her. I can't imagine life without her, and I feel full of hope for the future. For both our futures.

"They made my life hell"

I heard the crack of a branch snapping and my heart leapt into my throat. Was there someone lurking behind the bushes? I couldn't tell.

I could see the lights of the dual-carriageway ahead of me. I only had to cross the footbridge, walk past the park and turn into Brompton Drive, then into our street. Just another ten minutes' walking and I'd be safe.

I thought of Jessie, waiting at home for me. I thought of Dad, working so hard in his new job, all the time worried to death about Mum. She'd be home soon, hopefully a lot more like her old self. I couldn't bear the idea of Mark's death tearing my whole family apart.

I thought of Craig, lovely Craig. At least *something*'s gone right in my new life, I thought gratefully. I've got the kind of boyfriend I never, ever thought I'd find. And a good friend too, in Anna.

What was that? Three muffled figures came out of a side road and stood directly in front of me. They were girls – I was sure of that, they weren't tall enough to be guys – but they had scarves and hats on so I couldn't swear it was anyone I knew. I thought I recognized Meg Tate's black coat . . . and wasn't that Karen Connor's distinctive red hair I could see tucked under a dark-coloured hat?

"What d'you want?" I said more confidently than I felt, as they were blocking my path.

No one said anything.

I tried to walk on, push through them, and then felt a shove in the small of my back that sent me sprawling into the gutter. My school bag went flying and I felt something – a boot, probably – catch my shoulder a glancing blow.

Muggers! I thought as I lay there, terrified, curling my arms round my head to protect it. Oh, no! What are they going to do to me? I haven't got any money.

I felt another cruel blow smash into my ribs and almost blacked out with the pain. I heard a groan and realized that it was me. Then a voice – was it one I recognized? – called "Enough!" and I heard footsteps running away.

For a few moments I just lay there, winded. Then, very slowly, very cautiously, I sat up, wincing. My bag was a few metres away. I got slowly to my feet, hobbled over to it and picked it up. It hadn't even been opened, so nothing was missing.

They weren't muggers, then, I thought, tears

springing to my eyes. I wasn't a random target. I'd been chosen, deliberately, as a victim. And it wasn't hard to guess who by.

Somehow, I managed to get home, peel off my wet clothes, and crawl into a hot bath. My tights were ruined, my school skirt was soaked and I was bruised all over, with one long graze on my leg. I lay in the hot, scented water, tears of shock and weariness streaming down my cheeks.

So much for starting a new life! I thought tiredly. It's every bit as bad out here as it was in London. It seems as though everywhere I go, there are people who hate me and want to make my life a misery. I can't stand it.

"Kerry? What in the world have you done to yourself?" Dad said when he came home. I was in my dressing-gown, still looking battered and bruised and feeling sick and miserable.

For a moment I was tempted to tell Dad all about it. Perhaps he could do something, or the school. . .

But then I thought of Valerie Maxwell's reaction if she knew I'd grassed, and shuddered. If my life was hell now, what would it be like after that?

No, I couldn't tell Dad. Anyway, he had enough to worry about with Mum. This was something I had to sort out myself.

"I fell over," I said. "Slipped on some wet leaves on my way home. I've given my ribs a bit of a bashing."

"Let me see."

I showed Dad the bruises and he was horrified, but seemed to accept my story that I'd had a bad fall. He put some ointment on them and tucked me up in bed with a bowl of tomato soup and some toast, just as if I was a little girl again. Jessie came and sat comfortingly on the bed beside me, her nose resting on her paws.

Dad made me stay off school the next day. Then I went back and carried on as if nothing had happened. I'd told Anna, of course, and Craig, but there was nothing any of us could do. I'd thought I'd recognized Meg's coat and Karen's red hair, but that was all. Once, I caught Valerie looking at me with a smug gleam in her dark eyes, but that didn't prove anything either. Mostly, they all just ignored me, as before.

Oh, there were little annoyances, like my best pen disappearing as mysteriously as my gold chain had done, Amy Flowers tripping me up in gym class and swearing it was an accident, inkstains appearing on my new sports bag, someone writing NUTTER on a piece of paper and slipping it into my desk, loud remarks being made whenever Anna and I came into the room, but no one actually attacked me again.

"To think we thought she might have given up!" I said miserably to Craig.

Even he was looking worried by this time. He'd been furious when I told him about the attack and made me promise never to walk home alone again, even if it meant waiting an hour for the bus.

"Oh God, Kerry! I'm sorry," he said. "I feel as if half of this is my fault, anyway."

"Your fault? How can it be?"

"If I'd known that Valerie was going to terrorize the next person I went out with . . . I wish to God I'd never gone out with her at all!"

"It's not your fault," I assured him. "She's crazy, and the craziest thing is, she thinks this is the way to get you back."

When I felt really down, I even thought about splitting up with Craig, or at least pretending to, just to see if that would calm her down.

"It won't," Craig said gloomily. "Even if you and I really did split up, I'd never, *ever* go back to her, especially not after this. Anyway, I don't see why we should let her split us up. You're the best thing that's ever happened to me, Kerry."

I hugged him tight.

"So are you," I assured him.

He took my hand and held it tightly in his.

"We're not going to let her pull us apart, Kerry," he said. "We're not, are we?"

My hand looked small and pale next to his big tanned one. I managed a watery smile and held on more tightly.

"No," I said firmly. "Together, we're strong. Stronger than Valerie, stronger than anyone."

"Together," he echoed.

***

At school that week Valerie, Meg and Karen were full of the weekend trip they'd made to London. They'd been to Camden Lock and Portobello Road and out clubbing every night. Valerie, at least, had come back with tonnes of new clothes and, according to Karen, had pulled an incredibly good-looking guy. She would! I thought, but I didn't say anything. London, and the life I'd led there, seemed like a million years ago. I didn't even feel envious. London made me think about Mark, and even after all these months, it still hurt. My life was here now, with Craig, and Anna, Mum and Dad – and Jessie.

I was only half-listening when Valerie and the others were talking about their trip to Judy and Amy, who'd stayed at home. It was only when I heard my name mentioned that my attention was really grabbed.

Meg had lowered her voice but I could still hear her. I looked over at the gossiping crowd and sighed to myself, expecting some bitchy comment at any moment.

Judy's eyes were like saucers.

"Are you sure it's true?" she was saying.

Meg and Valerie both nodded.

"No wonder she hardly ever talks about him," said Karen in a loud voice.

Valerie looked up, caught my eye, and said casually, "How come you didn't tell us about your brother, Kerry?"

I felt cold inside.